The Forbidden Secrets of the Goody Box

By

Valerie J. Lewis Coleman

Published by

Pen of the Writer, LLC
Dayton, Ohio
PenOfTheWriter.com

Published by

Pen of the Writer, LLC
Dayton, Ohio
PenOfTheWriter.com

Library of Congress Control Number: 2010902982

ISBN-13: 978-0-9786066-3-3
ISBN-10: 0-9786066-3-9
E-book ISBN-13: 978-0-9786066-6-4
E-book ISBN-10: 0-9786066-6-3

Cover design by Candace K
Edited by Wendy Hart Beckman
Proofread by Lynel Johnson Washington
Author photo by Branham Photography

Printed in the United States of America

Praise for The Forbidden Secrets of the Goody Box...

"A brilliant writer. I love her work. The characters are so real, so rich and fleshed out so well. You hit the nail on the head with these women. Can I have the rights to the movie?"
~ Mother Love, TV and Radio show host of *The Mother Love Show*

"I started to skim through this book, but now I cannot put it down. This is an incredible book that all women must read."
~ Lexi, talk-show host of *The Lexi Show* as seen on The Word Network

"Coleman lays the hard-hitting arsenal out in the open in this refreshing and looong-awaited new spin on an ageless battle to tame the flesh! *Goody Box* is not just a novel, but a woman's must-have, must-READ handbook full of great teachings and insight on reaching personal and relational fulfillment. *Goody Box* will have you pledging heart-gasm before orgasm!"
~ Dr. Vivi Congress, author of *Manna for Mamma*

"In *The Forbidden Secrets of the Goody Box,* golden nuggets of relationship counseling, neatly sandwiched between candid conversations only shared with friends, offer a healing balm for persons hiding behind broken hearts and shattered dreams."
~ Andrea Attaway-Young, author of *The Secret Treasure*

Dedication

This book is dedicated to the little girl in every woman.

Acknowledgments

Special thanks to my team of *Goody Box* readers: Mary Allen, Tonya Baker, Shakena Campbell, Dr. Vivi Monroe Congress, Sheila Green, Barbara Hurd, Serida Lowery and Arvena Montague and proofreader extraordinaire: Pat "Hawkeye" Bray.

Chapter 1

For the Love of Vincent

Sunday-morning service stirred Debra Hampton's heart. The poignant message convinced her to resolve a matter that had her torn for almost a year. She had been undecided about whether to marry her live-in boyfriend, Vincent. He didn't share her religious beliefs and refused to go with her to church, but she knew that he was the best man for her. He laughed at her silly antics, talked with her about her ambitions and encouraged her to greatness. He made her the focal point of his life and involved her in every decision no matter how minute. But it was his touch that held her hostage, kept her toying with God's love by giving herself to a man who was not her husband.

With her head bowed to hide the free-flowing tears, she exited the church without speaking to anyone. She sat in her Mercedes S550, took a moment to freshen her makeup, expelled a sigh of relief. She looked to Heaven through the panorama sunroof, smiled, closed her eyes, gave thanks. The decision to accept Vincent's proposal resonated; filled her with peace as she trusted the Lord with her soul mate.

The thirty-minute drive from the inner-city church to her suburban home gave her ample time to reflect upon the life they would build together: three children, business partnership and unlimited mind-blowing sex. The rush of blood to her southern bell—the name her mother called her vagina when she was a child—gave her pause. Fortunately, she was stopped at a red light. She clicked through the Sirius Satellite stations and then opted to enjoy tunes Vincent had downloaded to her iPod a few nights prior.

As she turned into Creekwood Estates—a lavish community north of Dayton—she admired the mansion-sized homes set hundreds of feet from the street. Manicured lawns featured rows of exotic trees, shrubbery and blooming flowers. Cobblestone driveways boasted luxury cars and backyards had customized gym sets or in-ground pools.

Her stucco and brick palatial home was small in comparison to those of her neighbors, but it was big enough for her family-to-be. She loved the side-entry, three-car garage because it camouflaged the unpacked moving boxes from passersby. She parked in the usual spot—closest to the mudroom door—and then she smiled wide. "He's home."

Debra grabbed her purse and Bible and then jaunted into the house. She placed her belongings on the granite countertop, careful not to make noise. Since the television wasn't locked on a sporting event, Vincent had to be resting in the master suite. A 3,500-square-foot home and he preferred the family room and bedroom.

She slipped off her stilettos, tiptoed up the stairs. Her heart beat faster with each step. She wiped her palms together to dry the sweaty moisture, pressed her ear to the door. His subtle snores seeped through. She giggled and then covered her mouth to halt the escape of more laughter.

She opened the door, peeked in, swung it wide. "Vincent! What the devil?"

"Debra, what are you doing here?" After a quick dismount, he rummaged the floor for his Fruit of the Looms. "When'd you get home?"

"Who is this woman and why is she in *my* bed?" She ran to the side of the bed, towered over her betrayer. Breath stalled in her throat, eyes widened. "Catherine!"

Catherine—the first person to welcome Debra to the neighborhood—reached for her clothes, scurried to dress.

Debra lunged at her, snatched her by the ponytail, drew back her fist. Just as she connected with Catherine's right jaw, Vincent grabbed Debra around the waist, pulled her away. She flailed her arms, kicked at his shins, head-butted him in the mouth. When he released her, she pursued Catherine who was halfway down the stairs, underwear in tow.

Debra leapt from the top stair, using Catherine as a landing pad. Spewing expletives, she pummeled her in the back of the head, until Vincent pulled her off.

He tightened his grip on Debra's arms, spun her around to look him in the eyes. "Stop it!" A trickle of blood oozed from the corner of his mouth.

"I cannot believe you had that female up in *my* house." The same channels that had released tears of joy now flooded her face in sadness. "Vincent, how could you?" She watched Catherine sprint through the backyard; battered, bruised and butt-naked.

"I tried to tell you, but—"

"You tried to tell me what? The last thing I knew, you were looking for an engagement ring."

"I was…for Catherine."

Debra's head danced like a bobble-head doll, her vision blurred. Her body quivered and then went slack as she collapsed in Vincent's arms.

~ ~ ~ ~ ~ ~ ~

A few minutes later, Debra awoke on the family-room couch. She picked up the note that set on the table.

> *Debra,*
> *I'm sorry you had to find out like this. I'll be back to get my things. I love you, but not enough to make you my wife.*
> *Vincent*

As she let the note float to the floor, the back door opened and then closed. The man whom she was willing to love forever had tiptoed out of the house and driven out of her life.

The agony of unreciprocated love left Debra in despair. Virtual restrainers confined her to the bedroom—the viaduct of deceit. She cried until her body heaved and the reservoir of tears was empty.

Chapter 2

Wallow

Depression infiltrated Debra and she withdrew into an abyss of desolation. She called off from work using a flare-up of Crohn's disease as the reason. Given that her body responded with similar symptoms—loss of appetite, abdominal cramps, fatigue and diarrhea—she resolved that it was a legitimate excuse for at least a week of sick days.

Unable to lie on the bed stained with the passion of another, she walked through the French doors that separated the bedroom from the sitting room: her "Me Time" room. On chilly nights, she'd cozy up in the oversized chair next to the crackling fireplace, sip on hot chocolate and admire the wooded backyard through the picture window. On occasion, deer emerged to nibble on bark.

Debra rested on the chair and would have slept away her sorrows but for the fact that memories of Vincent invaded her dreams. When she tired of the torment, she forced herself to walk past the bed to the walk-in closet. She changed out of her church clothes into black satin pajamas. The soft material alleviated the itchy sensation that spread across her arms and legs like poison ivy on a scantily dressed trail hiker: a side effect of stress.

As she stood in the closet, she looked at herself in the full-length mirror. She rationalized that her actions caused this life disruption. "Why did I come home early? My life would be so much easier." She bowed her head, released a sigh from the depths of her belly, cried.

She wiped the tears with the back of her hand and noticed Vincent's dress shirts—pressed with light starch—hanging on wooden hangers. She stared at the array of shirts, most of which she had purchased. She caressed her face with each shirt, inhaled hoping to get a whiff of his scent: Dolce & Gabbana. She slid her size-six feet into his favorite dress shoes and then reached for a necktie. When she contemplated using it as a noose to dangle strange fruit from the loft balcony, she fell to the floor. After a minute or so of unbridled tantrum, she sat up, pulled her knees to her chest, rocked back-and-forth, side-to-side. The movement lulled her into a brief nap.

Having relaxed the tension in her neck, her head jerked and startled her awake. She left the comfort of the closet floor only to be assaulted by a recall of Vincent and Catherine. Unwilling to revisit the experience with each glance of the bed, she made the arduous trek to the family room. She grabbed the trashcan from the powder room in case her dry heaves manifested into something more than mini-convulsions and then positioned herself on the couch.

She skimmed through the channels, but didn't see anything to complement her melancholy mood so she let reruns on the *Lifetime* channel keep watch over her.

Debra alternated between bouts of nightmarish sleep, crying and reminiscing. She recalled Vincent's attentiveness. He loved to cook. He often had dinner prepared and the table set when she walked in the door. And on those days when the demands of the job overwhelmed her, he massaged her feet, caressed her hands, made love to her.

In return for his passion, she upgraded him. Lavished him with expensive gifts, exposed him to exclusive restaurants, fine arts and music. He often traveled with her on business trips and enjoyed the lifestyle of the rich and famous at the expense of her clients: first-class airfare when private jets weren't available, five-star hotels, limousine service and meals by world-renowned chefs. While Debra prepared for trial, Vincent spent her money on clothes, cologne and probably Catherine.

Instead of bringing her a semblance of peace, the memories served only as weapons of destruction. How could he love her the way she wanted and needed to be loved, yet give his heart to another? Why wasn't her love enough? What could she have done differently? Where did she fall short?

When the house phone rang, Debra let it roll over to voicemail. She turned off her cell, disconnected her laptop. Like a tree planted by the water, Debra took root on that couch and left only to relieve her bladder.

~ ~ ~ ~ ~ ~ ~

Debra was startled by the rattle of the garage door opening.

"Oh, no. Vincent is coming to get the rest of his things." She sat up on the couch, contemplated hiding and then decided to stay and fight for her man.

A loud, female voice echoed from the kitchen. "Ms. Dee! Where are you?"

Debra rolled her eyes, slumped on the couch. "In here." *Why didn't I change the code on that garage door?*

Her girlfriends, Rachel and Sherry, bounded into the room

like they were on a reconnaissance mission. The trio met in college during freshmen orientation and melded instantly. Each had aspirations to graduate, travel the world and then settle into the traditional roles of wife and mother, but only Rachel had succeeded in fulfilling all of the objectives. She met her husband, Brian, at a Greek event on campus. The statuesque pair resembled models from Ebony Fashion Fair. They married a few years after graduation and their wedding photo was featured in *Jet*. Brian's romantic gestures and Rachel's nurturing ways inspired Debra to believe that true love is attainable. In contrast, the couple's compatibility sickened her because it reminded her of her unfinished business—mid-thirties, single and no hopeful prospects—a torturous type of purgatory for a project-oriented person.

Sherry was the conservative one in the group. Frivolous spending during her college tenure left her with lots of credit-card debt and student loans. Although she paid off the debt years ago, she committed to never live beyond her means. She survived off half her net pay and banked the rest. Her modestly furnished one-bedroom apartment was within the city limits. Her used 2002 Monte Carlo was reliable and paid in full. She shopped for clothes twice a year, buying quality versus trendy. Makeup and hair-care products were purchased from Wal-Mart. She became an expert do-it-yourselfer from changing a flat tire to fixing a leaky toilet to doing her own hair which she set in tight curls. She washed and set her hair Saturday nights and then slept with the rollers to have full locks for Sunday. She combed her hair by running her fingers through it—oftentimes the parts from rolling her hair were still visible. The remainder of the first week following a shampoo, she slept in a satin bonnet and styled her hair using the same finger-comb technique. Week two, she combed and wrapped her hair. The process gave her hair body that lasted until the next shampoo; not a complimentary look, but a cost-effective time saver.

Rachel walked to the customized drapes that shrouded the floor-to-ceiling window. "Girl, if you don't open the drapes and let in some sun. It looks like a cave in here."

A gurgle rattled in Debra's throat. She shielded her face with her arms as if the light would singe her flesh.

Sherry pinched her nose. "And it smells like one, too." She sniffed toward Debra. "Is that you?" She covered her mouth, gagged. "That is so nasty."

Rachel hit Sherry on the shoulder. "Have some compassion. This is tough on her."

With a hint of sarcasm, Sherry said, "I know. Been in this place many times myself." Her tone mellowed. "But coddling her is not the solution." She turned to Debra, rubbed her back. "You have got to get out of this funk. You haven't been to work in almost a we—"

Debra grabbed her stomach. "It's these cramps."

"Uh huh. As I was saying, you look awful, smell worse."

"Is this your way of making her feel better?"

"Is what she's doing now going to make her feel better? Look at her." She pointed to Debra as if she were a freak at a side-show carnival. "Her dark, puffy eyes look like a football player with that black stuff on his face." Sherry tried to comb her fingers through Debra's coal-black hair which cascaded mid-way down her back: an attribute of her Cherokee heritage. "Her hair is so matted, my hand is stuck. Tell me that's okay with you and I'll let it go." She cocked her head to the right, waited for Rachel's response. "Her acne has flared up and don't tell me that you are not offended by how she smells. That is a-w-f-u-l!"

Debra rolled over on the couch, turned her back to her friends.

"See what you did," Rachel snapped, as she rubbed Debra's arm. "We are supposed to be consoling her."

"I am not an enabler." She tugged on Debra's arm. "Come on, girl. It's time to shake this off."

Debra jerked away. "Leave me alone."

"Can't do that. I love you too much to let you let Vincent get the best of you."

Like a ventriloquist, Rachel's lips barely moved as she said, "You are not supposed to say his name." She punched Sherry.

Sherry cut her eyes at Rachel. "That was your last pass. One more punch and it's going to go all wrong up in here." She grabbed Debra's arm. With each mention of the assailant, she tried to pull Debra off the couch. "*Vincent* is not worth it. *Vincent* can go back to the hole he crawled out of. *Vincent* is going to regret the day he played you. *Vin*—"

Debra looked up at Sherry, tears brimmed her eyes. "Why are you being so mean to me?"

"You're not going to be able to avoid him or his name."

Rachel started to punch Sherry, but then remembered the promise, withdrew her hand. "So you're going to beat her over the head with his name to desensitize her?"

"If that's what you want to call it. We run in the same circles. She's going to cross paths with Vincent," she tugged on Debra. "And I don't want her to crumble when she does. It's time to gird up her loins for warfare."

"Oh, Lord. You're pushing her to fight mode and she's still in the oh-woe-is-me phase. Give her time to recover."

"And how long is that? Another couple of weeks? By then she'll have lost her job, her mind and her hair. I'm not trying to make her suppress the pain, just work through it. She can't stop living because Vincent is a self-absorbed, good-for-nothing, high-paid gigolo who skeeted and screeched!" She snatched Debra off the couch, stared into her eyes. "Now, we are going upstairs so that you can take a bath; a very long bath. Do you need me to put you in the tub or can you do it yourself?"

A tear trickled down Debra's cheek, she expelled a deep sigh. "I can do it."

"Very good." Sherry commended her like a schoolmarm with a pre-schooler and patted her on the head.

Debra shrugged, lowered her head and then turned toward the stairs. Sherry walked behind her.

"I said that I can do it myself."

"And I know that you can. I'm just coming for moral support." She smiled. "I want to hear the Jacuzzi running. You need to let that water work its way into every nook and cranny."

Debra walked into the master suite. She paused, looked at the king-sized bed that clung to the evidence of the exchange of bodily fluids.

Sherry said, "How about we buy a new mattress set and sheets?"

"That would be nice." With slow, somber steps, she entered the bathroom.

Sherry brushed past Debra, turned up her nose. She started the bath water, reached for the bubble bath. "I'm going to add a little extra Bath and Body Works." She waved her hand under the running water to test the temperature. "You are going to feel so much better."

"If you say so."

"I promise." Sherry lit three candles, exited the bathroom, closed the door. She walked into the sitting room, turned on the Bose sound system and put Kirk Franklin's *He Will Take the Pain Away* on repeat. The music piped through the ceiling and wall-mounted speakers. She looked at the tropical fish in the small aquarium set on a Pulaski pedestal near the chaise lounge. "I'm surprised you guys aren't belly up." She sprinkled a little food in the water.

Debra stared in the mirror. She had put a lot of energy into designing the bathroom when her home was under construction. Imported marble encased the countertops, walls and floors. His-and-hers vessel sinks formed from weathered bronze were mounted on opposite sides of the vanity. Expensive Mikasa vases—which normally caressed fresh-cut flowers—displayed lifeless potpourri. The walk-in shower that was large enough for a basketball team hadn't been used since Vincent took her away to ecstasy three days before the ultimate fighting match.

She sighed, wiped the crust from her eyes and then disrobed. She tossed her panties in the vanity trashcan, stepped into the two-person Jacuzzi that was flanked on both sides by Roman-like pillars. She sank into the warm water, submerged until only her face peeked through.

While Debra soaked away the stench and sadness, her friends packed Vincent's clothes. Although he had mooched off her for several months, he traveled light. It only required two Hefty lawn-and-leaf bags to hold the stuff he had brought over from the make-shift apartment in his mother's basement. His exclusive attire acquired from Boutique a la Debra took a few more bags.

Rachel knocked on the bathroom door. "You okay in there?" When she didn't get an answer, she cracked open the door, spoke louder. "Debra, you okay?"

"Yeah, I'm good."

Rachel closed the door, nodded at Sherry. "I'm going to drop these off to Goodwill."

"Some well-deserving man is going to look fabulous in these Armani suits." Sherry rapped on the door. In a sing-song voice, she said, "I don't hear the Jacuzzi."

Debra sat up, pressed the button, reclined back on the tub wall.

"The world thanks you for cleaning your tail."

Rachel shook her head. "You are so crass."

"Better crass than smelly...."

"Awful."

Chapter 3

A Monroe Mourning

Rachel and Brian were the typical married couple: monotonous routines, average sex and frequent irritants. The team that promised to love, honor and overtake the world had settled into an existence of semi-contentment and sedentary adventure. Much like slowly boiling a frog to death without its knowing, the years had overcooked the passion and purpose of their marriage. They had achieved the "American dream" having acquired a lot of STUFF— Some Things Used For the Flesh—but missed the mark on "happily ever after."

Rachel had become disenchanted with her college sweetheart. She didn't need her knight to build her a palace or shower her with gifts—her parents taught her to avoid the demise of a damsel in distress—but when she needed her heroic warrior to protect her from the fire-breathing dragon, ravenous pillagers and pre-queen concubines, he fell off his horse during the joust. Apparently Brian was out on a Robin-Hood run when Sir Lancelot taught the knighthood principles of loyalty, courage and honor.

The couple was sprawled on opposite sides of the king-sized sleigh bed. The bronze-colored imported silk that canopied the bed, also draped the windows. Per his customary modus operandi, Brian tested the murky moat waters. He slid across the drawbridge, placed his hands between her legs, massaged her inner thighs.

She moved his hand. "Not this morning, babe."

"It's been three weeks."

"No it hasn't. We just had sex last week."

"No, Rach. The last time we had sex was on my birthday."

"Are you sure?"

"Yeah, a brother doesn't forget something like that." He caressed her back, kissed her neck, moved in close.

"Brian." She scooted forward to put distance between her behind and his bulging javelin.

"The alarm hasn't even gone off yet. I only need five minutes."

Although Rachel was far from being an "experienced" woman, she knew how she wanted to be pleasured. She had had two partners who took her to places she could only relive in her dreams. They had studied her body, knew its intricacies, enjoyed her response. Brian, however, try as he might, couldn't bring her to the point of release as he once could. She took responsibility for her part in the problem and accepted that she had emasculated her husband with her lifeless reaction to his gyrations. She found the daunting task mundane and made no attempt to cooperate unless she wanted to expedite the process. The slightest move of her pelvis and he spilled his seed.

The couple had tried to work through the sexual tension by scheduling sex for Monday nights. That worked until football season and then Brian wanted to switch to Thursdays. Inconvenient for Rachel because of all the running around she did with the kids, she tried to oblige her husband with what she referred to as duty booty. But as the 'S' on her Super Woman cape faded, so did her libido and what was once a daily treat she often initiated, became a chore she dreaded.

"You know I hate it when you wake me up. I don't sleep well as it is and you insist on interrupting what little bit of rest I do get."

"Come on, girl. You're up now and wasting time talking about what you don't have time to do."

She got out of bed, stretched, yawned and then began her morning routine. She pet Mogli, the family's American Cocker Spaniel. He trotted into the bathroom behind her.

Brian rolled over and stuffed his manhood back into his boxers. "What about tonight?"

"Huh?"

Brian walked into the bathroom, leaned on the doorframe. "Can I get some tonight?"

Rachel sighed, rolled her eyes, turned up her lip.

"Why do you have to make that face?"

"I have a lot to do today. By the time I get home, feed the kids and check their homew—"

"I'm working from home today, so what can I do to help?"

As she brushed her teeth, she said, "Charisse has gymnastics at the daycare. She'll be done twirling at six-thirty. I'll drop her off on my way to work, but I need you to pick her up."

"Okay."

"Marcus has a field trip to the Art Institute. They'll be back in time to catch the bus home from school, but I need you to meet him at the bus stop at three-thirty." She spit and then rinsed.

Brian walked to the toilet. He lifted the seat, relieved his bladder. "He's six years old. He can walk five blocks home."

She glared at Brian, tightened her lips. "I told you those kids are picking on him. Until I can talk with the school and the parents of those hoodlums, I don't want him walking home. Is that okay with you?"

"When I was a kid, I had to…" He looked up from the porcelain king to see Rachel staring at him.

She put more bass in her voice. "Is that okay with you?"

"Cut the apron strings." He flushed. "I'll get him."

Rachel cleared her throat.

Brian lowered the seat and then walked to the sink to wash his hands.

"Just because we call him Marcus Aurelias Marcus the King doesn't mean he's running things." She rolled her eyes. "BJ has soccer practice from five to seven. I can't get him there or pick him up today."

"So you need me to do both?"

"Yeah, unless you feel that he can walk the five miles there and back. I mean he's almost a man at eight." She disrobed, stepped into the shower.

Brian spoke louder to be heard above the oversized Kohler Rain Shower showerhead. "You really need to calm down. It's not that big of a deal. If he's late or misses practice, the team will be fine."

"What values are you trying to teach our children? He wanted to play and now he's going to give it his best. No slacking. The Monroes aren't bred from that kind of stock."

"And you know that because…?"

"I really don't have time for this right now."

"Well, if you'd carry my name, we wouldn't have to rehash this."

"Brian, I do carry your name."

"On paper only."

"Well, that's where it's most important."

"Not to me. I want people to know that you're my wife."

She opened the shower door, peeked out. "Can you pass me the shampoo?"

Brian looked under the sink, handed her the shampoo.

"What were you saying? Oh yeah, they do know."

"Yeah, but they think my name is Brian Nance. You know how frustrating that is? Even the kids at church refer to me as Brother Rachel. What is that?"

Rachel giggled.

"It's not funny."

"I'm sorry. That is so cute to me."

"And that's the problem. It's not cute at all."

"Brian, you know how important this company is to me; to us. RJ Nance Marketing is our bread and butter."

"Now you want to insult my manhood. I work, too."

"Babe, I know you do. I'm just saying the business brings in almost seventy percent of our household income."

"Here we go."

"Without that money, we couldn't live like this."

"Now my money ain't enough?"

"You are twisting my words. I branded RJ Nance long before you asked me to marry you. I'm the face of the company. It's more than just a name change. It has a ripple effect that I'm not willing to deal with right now." She stepped out of the shower, dried off, wrapped the towel around her hair.

"It's been eleven years. When will you be ready to deal with it?" Brian admired her slender body which glistened with tiny droplets of water. Except for a few stretch marks on her hips, her body looked exactly as it did when he first saw her naked. They dated exclusively for almost two years before she granted him access to her diamond mine. He jiggled to get his manliness under control.

"I cannot believe that you are so focused on this. You know that I'm still trying to salvage the mess that Bob made when he left the company." She shook her head. "After all I did for him, he goes and starts his own firm, taking one-third of my clients with him."

"Have you figured out what you're going to do?"

"I have a few things planned. The office manager has really been helpful." She slipped into a red business suit with a skirt that hugged the curvature in her hips. "He stepped up and volunteered to call each client in a non-threatening manner. He's taking a survey to solicit feedback as to why they left."

"Good idea." Brian patted her butt.

She shooed off his love tap. "That's what I told him. It shows our commitment to them and concern for the lost business without condemning Bob. So far," she crossed her fingers, "it's been effective in drawing some of them back."

"Good stuff."

"What's the weather going to be like today?"

"Mid-70s."

"Cool. I can let my hair air dry."

"Yeah, I like it when you wear it like that."

"Thanks." Barelegged, she slid into her stilettos. "I taught Bob a lot, but not everything. With the tricks I have up my sleeve and the office manager's ingenuity, I'll recover most of the clients and garner new ones." She chuckled. "Not to mention the fact that Bob does not have the people skills to pull this stunt off on an on-going basis. He'll have one of his outbursts and that'll be the end of that."

Brian looked at the clock. "It's seven. Are the kids up?"

"Oh, Lord. Can you check for me? I have to be out of here in twenty minutes or I'll be late for my first meeting."

Rachel applied brown eyeliner and finishing powder.

Brian left the bathroom and then returned. "Everyone's up and moving."

"Good. You let Mogli out to pee?" Thirteen years ago, Rachel offered to provide temporary boarding to help out Debra's niece, Aisha. Her parents had moved into a non-pet-friendly apartment months after Aisha received the puppy as a birthday gift. The act of generosity became a lifelong love and commitment as Aisha's family didn't come back for Mogli.

Rachel kept his buff-and-white coat cut low instead of the traditional high-maintenance American Cocker-Spaniel skirt. She didn't have time to run her fourth baby to the groomer every couple of weeks.

"He's outside now."

"Good." Rachel walked into the kitchen. She pulled the kids' lunches out of the refrigerator and mated them with the appropriate backpacks: Batman for BJ, Pokémon for King Marcus and Uniqua of the *Backyardigans* for Charisse. She boiled a teapot of water and then microwaved a pack of turkey bacon. She poured each child's preferred brand of instant hot breakfast into a bowl. As she waited for the teapot to whistle, she loaded the Honda Pilot with her briefcase, purse and Charisse's things. She walked back in the house.

Rachel received great satisfaction in being a mother. She kept the kids active, focused and respectful. She believed that an occupied child is an entrepreneur in the making. Team activities instilled discipline, hard work, commitment and more. To keep them grounded and benevolent, she involved them in feeding the homeless on holidays, donating used clothes and toys and participating in the children's ministry at her church.

Brian had corralled the kids to the table.

"Good morning, Mommy," they chimed in unison.

"Good morning, Mommy's babies." She hugged and kissed her little ones, giving each her undivided attention. "How did you sleep?"

Per usual, BJ spoke first. "I slept okay, but Marcus plays too much." He punched his brother in the arm.

"Owww. Mommy, he hit me again."

"BJ, I know you know better than that. Now tell your brother you're sorry and give him a hug."

"But Mom—"

"No buts. He's got enough folks picking on him. He doesn't need his big brother on his back, too. You're supposed to protect your brother." She heard Mogli scratching on the back door.

"I do protect him. Those kids don't mess with him when I'm there. They know better."

"Very good." She rubbed his head, walked to the back door, spoke over her shoulder. "I didn't hear you apologize."

"Sorry Marcus." He leaned over and hugged his sibling.

When Rachel opened the door, Mogli jumped up and his front paws landed on her thighs. In a sing-song voice, Rachel said, "Hey, Stink Mogli. How's Momma's baby?" She rubbed him and tickled the back of his ears. She grabbed a Pupperoni snack. "Here's your good-boy treat." She dangled the snack in the air and snickered as Mogli danced on his hind legs to get it.

Charisse—the unplanned Monroe child—was not going to be upstaged by her brothers. "Mommy, I got to potty."

Rachel helped her three-year-old baby girl to the bathroom. "Did Daddy put you on the potty when you got up?"

"No, ma'am."

Rachel rolled her eyes, assisted Charisse. "Here's the

toilet paper."

"Thank you, Mommy." She looked up at her mother with beautiful, brown, almond-shaped eyes. "Front to back."

"Very good, baby. Wipe your 'gina from front to back." Rachel picked up Charisse, propped her baby on her right knee, balanced on her left high heel. They sang a full verse of *Old McDonald Had a Farm* to make sure her little hands were clean.

"Okay, precious. Go eat breakfast so we can get you to school." She patted Charisse on her bottom.

"I'm Uniqua."

"Okay, Uniqua. Go eat."

While the kids finished eating, Rachel prepared her breakfast. She grabbed a packet of Weight-Control Instant Cream of Wheat and poured it into a plastic to-go container. "Brian, can I talk to you in the other room?"

She walked to the living room with Brian in close pursuit. Rachel spoke in a low voice. "How is it that you can remember the last time we had sex, but you can't remember to take your daughter to the bathroom?"

He sighed. "I'm sorry, babe. I forgot."

"You forgot? What if she had peed on herself? I don't have time to redo stuff. I need you to work with me."

"Okay, okay. She didn't pee on herself so what's the problem?"

"The problem is I feel like I'm doing everything by myself." She looked at the partially painted room, flung her arms. "See, what I mean? You promised to have this room done weeks ago."

"I told you that I'd get around to it and I will."

"When, Brian? When will you get around to it?"

"I—"

"Do you have the kids' itineraries or do you need me to

draft yet another to-do list?" She sucked air in through her teeth.

"I know how to take care of my kids."

"Uh huh."

Charisse called from the kitchen. "Mommy, I made a boo-boo."

"We'll finish this later." Rachel brushed past Brian to resolve yet another problem.

Marcus stood next to his sister. He wiped the front of her shirt with a Bounty paper towel. "She spilled a little milk from her sippy cup."

"Thanks, big boy." She rubbed his head, felt Charisse's shirt, knelt to look in her eyes. "Uniqua, you're Mommy's big girl and you have to be careful with your milk, right?"

"Yes, Mommy." She smiled. Her full, round cheeks looked like Alvin, Simon or Theodore with a mouthful of nuts.

Rachel smiled. "That's my girl." She stood. "Okay, guys. Grab your things and let's head to the SUV. Chop, chop." Rachel stirred lukewarm water into her to-go instant breakfast and put a banana in her pocket. She tossed Mogli another good-boy treat and bounded out the door.

The kids fell into formation like military soldiers and took their respective places in the backseat of the Honda Pilot. Not the most expensive SUV, Rachel selected this vehicle for its features and reliability. It had plenty of room for her kids and a couple of her neighbors', cubbyholes for equipment and storage trays for Happy Meals. Rachel's favorite was the camera that displayed what's behind the car when it's in reverse: a must-have for any mom on the go.

"Come on, prec… I mean Uniqua. Let's get you in the car seat."

Charisse lifted up her arms. When Rachel picked her up,

she wrapped her legs around her mother's waist and gave her a butterfly kiss on the cheek.

"Thank you, baby." She put her in the car seat, fastened it, tugged on the seatbelt to ensure it was secure, kissed her on the forehead. She leaned into the SUV to kiss the boys, tugged on their seatbelts and touched each hand. "Protection in the name of Jesus."

She arrived at the bus stop just in time to see the bus rounding the corner. "All right guys, the bus is here. Have a good day.

"Yes, ma'am."

She looked at the boys through the rearview mirror. "Your daddy will be here to meet you, King Marcus." She clicked on the flashers. "And BJ, Daddy's going to get you to practice."

"Okay."

"You show those kids why we call you Super, okay?"

He smiled wide, got his things and waited for his brother. Except for his darker complexion, BJ looked exactly like his father and both boys walked like him: shoulders back, head titled slightly to the right and a minute hesitation when the right foot struck the ground.

Rachel and Charisse waved as the bus drove by. "Okay, Chunky Cheeks, let's go."

"Uniqua."

"My bad." Rachel turned on the radio to catch Tom, Sybil and J Anthony hamming it up on WROU 92.1 FM. The show was her calm before the work storm. She was three minutes from the office when Charisse sang *It's the God in Me* with Mary Mary. Rachel made a u-turn in the middle of the street, popped in a TinyTunesMusic.net CD—personalized with Charisse's name in each song—headed to the daycare.

I have to do better.

Chapter 4

Nick Nack Paddy Whack

Sherry hated her job. Well not so much the job as her boss, Roxanne. Until a few months ago, she enjoyed working at Oracle. She started there almost seventeen years earlier as a college intern and received several promotions over the course of her career.

Sherry's bright smile and attractive personality brought a glimmer of light to the dismal work environment. As with many companies in Dayton, the economy had affected profits and major cuts were pending. Many of her friends had been released, relocated or resigned. Like rats bailing from a sinking ship, they scurried to find other opportunities before the city was saturated with under-qualified and overqualified applicants. She couldn't imagine having to deal with Roxanne the Vampiress and Nicholas the Nemesis at the same time.

Four years earlier, when Oracle was still a viable company and Sherry still sang in the church choir, she met Nicholas. Her pastor was asked to minister at the annual pastoral anniversary for No Greater Love Church. His speaking engagement committed the choir to sing A and B pre-sermonic selections. The director set up the song—*Safe in His Arms* as performed by Milton Brunson and the Thompson Community Singers—and then handed the microphone to Sherry. With her eyes closed and right hand raised, she ministered to the Lord.

At eleven o'clock, when the Tuesday-night service concluded, Sherry stood in the lobby chatting with a couple of choir members. A young lady from the host church approached her.

"Hi, Sis. I enjoyed that song."

Careful not to let pride become a prelude to destruction, a haughty spirit or fall from His grace, humility resonated through Sherry's heart. "It's all Him." Sherry pointed toward Heaven.

"Can I talk to you for a second?"

"Sure." Sherry followed the woman to a secluded corner.

"My name is Sheila."

"Hi, Sheila." Sherry extended her hand. "My name is Sherry, Sherry Harris."

"Nice to meet you. My friend over there," she pointed to the opposite corner, "wanted to know if you were seeing anyone."

Having spent most of her life in church, Sherry lived by Proverbs 18:22—*he who finds a wife, finds a good thing*—and made it a point to never initiate contact with a man, even if she thought he was single, sexy and saved. When the other females circled fresh meat like buzzards to road kill, she sat back and waited. The lady-like tactic presented her with occasional opportunities as would-be suitors sought her out after escaping the feeding frenzy.

Sherry turned in the direction of the finger. A dark-brown man with small eyes and close-cut hair stared back at her. He looked to be in his late twenties, average build, height and attire. Although she wasn't actively seeking companionship, the gesture flattered her.

"You talking about the guy in the grey suit?" She nodded in his direction.

"Yeah. His name is Nicholas. So?"

"So what?"

"So are you seeing anyone?"

"No, I'm not, but—"

"Great." She waved over Nicholas. "He's a great guy."

"That may be, but I'm no—"

"Nicholas, this is Sherry. Sherry, this is Nicholas." Sheila smiled as if satisfied that she had fulfilled her requirements and then walked away.

Nicholas said, "Hi, Sherry. Pleased to meet you."

Sherry hesitated, shifted her eyes right and then left. The last guy she met at this church claimed that he loved her. A couple months into the relationship, he left Sherry to marry his previous girlfriend. According to Sherry's resources, he disappeared during the ceremony. The expecting bride-to-be sent a search party who found him ducked away in the janitor's closet. "Hi, Nicholas."

"Forgive my methods. I didn't want to be disrespectful, so I asked my friend to break the ice."

"Disrespectful?"

"To your boyfriend or husband. A woman as beautiful and gifted as you has to be connected to someone."

She batted her eyes, allowed a faint grin to cross her lips. He wasn't Morris Chestnut, but he showed interest in her and that was good enough. Like many women, she had esteem issues that stemmed from childhood. Her father once told her, "If you can't be beautiful, then be smart." Although the comment forged her aspirations in academia, it stifled her self-worth.

"I appreciate the consideration. And since you're standing here talking with me, you know that the coast is clear." She smiled.

"So may I walk you to your car?"

"Sure."

~ ~ ~ ~ ~ ~ ~

Over the next few weeks, Sherry and Nick Nick—her term of endearment for the romantic interest—enjoyed a series of late-night phone conversations.

He worked as a third-shift security guard at Oracle—a job that Sherry helped him acquire. At three in the morning, when he could no longer fight off the boredom, he often called her to chat. On several occasions, he asked her to bring him something to eat. She questioned why he didn't pack his lunch, but after a brief banter, she slid out of bed and either filled a Tupperware container with leftovers or hit a late-night drive-through in her pajamas.

"Sherry, I didn't like the yellow dress you had on the other day."

"Why? I got a lot of compliments in that outfit."

"That's why I don't like it. It drew too much attention to your shape."

"Aw, that's so cute. You were jealous."

"I'm serious. That dress is not becoming of a woman who may be my wife."

"Your wife? It's a little soon to be talking marriage."

"Not to me. I'm ready to settle down and I want my wife to be modest."

"You mean homely?"

"Not homely, presentable. That's how my mom carries herself; a virtuous woman." The second of four sons, Nicholas learned about relationships by watching his father dominate his mother. He grew up in the church under the

36

sand-and-sandals doctrine that women are to be seen and not heard. He believed that jewelry, makeup and pants were signs of the Jezebel spirit, not realizing that the Biblical woman's sin was that of manipulation and not concern for personal appearance.

"Hmm."

"What?"

"Per your definition, I can look the part of a virtuous woman: skirt dragging the ground, granny stockings, sleeves that button at my palms and hair pulled back in a tight bun. But none of that makes me virtuous."

"Are you challenging me?"

"If that's what you want to call it. I'm nowhere near a flashy girl, so I don't get the energy you're sending my way. Amazing."

"What?"

"I've watched you break your neck staring at Third-and-Main hoochies as I'm driving down the street. Even caught you waving out the car window at one female. So I'm confused as to what you really want: a respectably dressed woman or one with more around-the-way appeal?"

"Come on now. I'm not trying to start anything. I just want my girl to be all mine. I don't want to fight some dude for looking or talking to you crazy, but if I have to defend your honor then I will."

"That is so sweet."

As their relationship ensued, Nicholas morphed into a man whose loving consideration became jealous insecurity. He had alienated her from friends and family, refused to give her messages when they called, disconnected the phone, tracked her mileage to make sure she didn't stray. He used the spare key that she had hidden under a faux rock to access the house when she wasn't home. Had it not been for his shoe treads in the freshly vacuumed carpet, Sherry wouldn't have known he had been there.

Battling her own demons of diminished confidence and with minimal dating experience, she tolerated his verbal and emotional attacks; however, she was not going to be a victim of physical abuse. She told Nick Nick, "The first time you hit me will be the last time." She had witnessed her father beat her mother for years—even stepped in to defend her mother on occasion.

Given he was a regular at his church and hoping to be considered for deacon training, Nicholas wanted to maintain the appearance of a good man, so he didn't stay overnight at Sherry's apartment the nights he was off work. He often threatened to leave Sherry for a more obliging woman, if she didn't take care of his needs. He talked her into doing things that disgusted her and after the deed was done, he made her kneel on the side of the bed. With the bedroom smelling of sex and semen running down her legs, he told her to pray for forgiveness.

She knew that fornication was a sin, but felt that the repetitious prayer of "Lord, we won't do it again" was hypocritical as they recited it two to three times a week. He pitched a fit when she told him that they should either stop having sex or stop sending up empty prayers, so she kept the concern to herself to hold onto her man.

One day Sherry had to make a trip to Sears in the Salem Mall to replace the tires on her Monte. She and Nicholas sat in her car in the lot closest to the auto-mechanic department.

"Nick Nick, come in here with me. I don't understand all that talk about tread life, radials and stuff."

"Girl, you can do it. I'm tired."

"But I need you to help me so I get the right tires."

He flipped down the sun visor, reclined the bucket seat.

"I'm going to sleep."

She touched his arm, whined, "Come on."

He sneered at her, hit the button to unlock the door. "Bounce."

Sherry got out of the car, careful not to slam the door and then walked into Sears.

The sales associate—who was busy with a customer—acknowledged her. "Good afternoon, ma'am. I have three customers ahead of you. I'll be with you as soon as possible."

"Thanks." Sherry wandered around the department hoping to find a display that offered some insight into how to buy tires.

About twenty minutes later, the gentleman assisted her with the purchase. He explained which tires would be best for her car given her driving habits and budget. The recommended brand happened to be on sale.

"God is good." Sherry reached for her checkbook.

"Are you a Christian?"

"Yes, I am. I love the Lord. And you?"

"I don't go to church anymore. Did you want the tire warranty for sixty-nine dollars? If you get a flat tire, we'll repair it for free."

"And if it's not repairable?"

"We'll apply twenty-five dollars toward the purchase of a replacement."

"Sure."

"Your total is $348.54."

Sherry wrote out the check. "Why don't you go to church any—"

Before she could finish the question, Nick Nick blurted from behind her, "What is taking you so long? It doesn't take an hour to buy four tires!" He slapped the countertop.

Sherry jumped. She looked at the salesman who was obviously intimidated by Nicholas' aggressive tone and posturing. His face had reddened and his hands shook. Sherry turned to Nicholas. "What is wrong with you? It has not been an hour and I'm almost done, so chill out." She tore the check out of the checkbook, handed it to the salesman.

Once the transaction was complete, Sherry scheduled a time to have the tires installed and balanced. She left out of the store, yapping at Nick Nick.

"I cannot believe you came in there and acted like that."

"You took too long. Was he hitting on you or something?"

"No!"

"Don't raise your voice at me."

She clicked the remote unlock, got in the car. "Excuse me, but you raised your voice first." She fastened her seatbelt, put the key in the ignition, revved the engine.

"You call yourself being mad?"

"Nicholas, you came in there, acted a fool and embarrassed me. You're so worried about how you look in the eyes of others you just blew your witness with that man. Based on how you just showed out, he'll never come to church." She put the car in gear. "I asked you to come inside with me, but you were soooooo tired. You're never too tired when you want sex." She rolled her eyes. "Heathen."

Nicholas smacked Sherry's right cheek. "You've lost your mind if you think you can talk to me like that."

She grabbed her face, trembled, whimpered.

"You made me hit you."

Although the sting from the slap was evidence of his assault, Sherry was stunned that he hit her. She experienced his mean and surly ways, but never expected things to escalate to this point.

As she drove him to his apartment, she contemplated how to retaliate, make good on her you-get-one-time-to-hit-me promise. She knew that if she didn't get out of the situation, it would happen again. With her cheek swollen and red, her focus was to get him out of the car. She sped down Shiloh Springs Road with one hand on the steering wheel, the other caressing her face.

When they arrived at the apartment he shared with his brother, he stepped out the car, closed the door, leaned inside the window, said, "Be here at nine-thirty to take me to work."

The salt water that streamed down her face irritated her skin. She looked at him and then turned to look out the front windshield. In a soft, yet commanding tone, she said, "That was your last time," and then drove away.

Sherry notified property management that she had a problem with a stalker. They changed the locks on her apartment that day. She contacted Guardian Home Security to schedule the installation of an alarm system.

Nicholas called a few times apologizing for hitting her, but when Sherry threatened to let his pastor know what he had done, his attempts to reconcile ceased. She knew that he didn't want to hinder his climb up the church ladder.

Chapter 5

Ebb and Flow

Although Debra had endured several horrendous relationships, her I'm-at-least-whole-enough-to-function-in-public recovery time for this breakup took almost three weeks. Having exhausted all of her sick days, good days and vacation days, she returned to work. She may have been overwhelmed, but she had the wherewithal to keep her job.

She meandered into the law firm of Greene, Harvin & Jordan. She was sure that her plans to make senior partner were thwarted by the Vincent saga.

The new paralegal said, "Hi, Ms. Hampton. Glad you're feeling better."

"Thanks." She muttered a few words under her breath, walked into her office, closed the door. She leaned back on the door, perused the room. She closed her eyes and let her mind drift to a happier time.

Seated at her desk a few months earlier, Debra reviewed her notes in preparation for court, when the janitor tapped on the door.

"Hey, Ms. Hampton."

"Hi, Jason." She looked at her watch. "I had no idea it was after nine."

"They shut down the office and left you here in the dark again, huh?"

"Yeah."

"Let me know if you need me to walk you to the car. That parking garage can be dangerous this time of night." He emptied the trash receptacle. "I'm going to turn on the hall lights. It's too dark up here."

Without looking up, she said, "Thanks, Jason." She smiled and then returned to her work. Debra put in many late nights at the firm for three reasons: to provide her clients with the best possible representation, impress the partners and keep her mind occupied. Her mother told her that the women in her family often experienced bouts of depression so to ward off the generational curse, Debra stayed busy.

Debra was startled by another tap on the door. She squealed.

"I'm sorry, babe. I didn't mean to scare you." Vincent stood in the threshold with a picnic basket in one hand and fresh-cut oriental lilies in the other.

Debra touched her chest to slow her racing heart; not from being startled, but from Vincent's romantic gesture. "Aw, you are so thoughtful."

"Couldn't have my girl sitting here alone. The freaks come out at night, especially downtown." He set the flowers on the desk, gave her an open-mouth kiss. "You hungry?"

"Of course."

"I figured as much. You haven't eaten since breakfast have you?"

"Not a thing."

"Good because I have lots of food." He opened the basket Debra purchased at Longaberger.com/JuliaScholz-Pinger and then spread the tablecloth on the floor. He removed two champagne flutes and a chilled bottle of Dom Pérignon.

"Ooooh, very nice." Debra came from around the desk, pressed the front of her skirt with her hands, sat on the floor.

He reached in the basket and pulled out two plates, a pair of eating utensils and linen napkins. He displayed them like Vanna White on *Wheel of Fortune*.

Debra giggled.

Vincent drew a white carton out of the basket, poured its contents on her plate.

"You know me so well. My favorite: shrimp fried rice."

"Only the best for my baby. And the crème de la crème. Drum roll please."

Debra rapped her manicured nails on the floor.

"New York-style cheesecake with chocolate swirls for dessert." He reached into the basket one last time. "Cleanliness is next to godliness." He presented her with a travel-sized container of hand sanitizer.

"A-mazing."

They laughed, enjoyed dinner and concluded the evening with Debra bent over the desk and Vincent behind her.

Debra shook away the memory. *Did he ever love me or was I just his skeet factory?* She pushed herself off the door, wandered to the desk, looked at the picture of her and Vincent posed cheek-to-cheek and then placed it face-down in the credenza. She slouched in the chair and stared at the diplomas, credentials and awards prominently displayed on the wall. She had hoped that reflecting on her accomplishments would validate her worth; it didn't.

The ringing phone startled her.

In a monotone voice, she said, "Debra Hampton, how may I help you?"

Cheer echoed through the receiver as Rachel said, "Hola, señorita. Como esta?"

"Hola, señora."

"How are you doing?"

"I'm okay."

"You don't sound okay."

"I have my good days and my bad days."

"And today?"

"Today's a bad day. I'm trying to move past the hurt, but everything reminds me of him."

"Love's emotional rollercoaster is a beast. I tried to get in the office to get the picture, but that new guy wouldn't let me in."

"Yeah, Marcellus is very protective of me."

"Interesting. I called to see if you wanted to meet for lunch."

"I'm not hungry, but I could use the time away from the office and this desk."

"Oh, yeah. That's where you guys did the wild thang."

"More times than I care to admit."

"So where do you want to meet?"

"How about Chipotle on Brown Street?"

"Cool. See you at noon."

~ ~ ~ ~ ~ ~ ~

As usual, Rachel was the first to arrive. She sat at a stool with a window view of the street. She set her purse on the adjacent stool and glared at everyone who asked, 'Is this seat taken?'

Debra walked in the rear entrance. She saw Rachel waving at her from the front of the restaurant.

Rachel stood, set her purse on the floor and then hugged Debra. They sat.

Rachel smiled. "You look great."

"Thanks. I'm a good student."

"I know it. You never know when you'll run into an ex, so you have to be runway ready at all times." She played with Debra's hair. "Does your hair grow overnight or what?"

"Seems like it."

"Are you going to get some chips and salsa?"

"Nah, I'm good. Can you get me a cup of iced water?"

"Sure."

"I'll hold your spot."

"Now don't get into any trouble. This lunch crowd is rowdy and your IQ is low."

"IQ?"

"Ignorance quotient."

Debra let a faint smile crease her lips, as Rachel stepped away to stand in the long line. Debra propped her elbows on the counter, rested her chin on entwined fingers. She didn't notice the man who set his burrito bowl on the counter and sat on Rachel's stool.

He took his fourth bite when she said, "Oh, sir, I'm sorry. My friend is sitting there."

"I'm not your friend."

"Excuse me?"

"You said that your friend is sitting here. I'm sitting here and I'm not your friend."

Her face contorted as she fought to hold back the words that rumbled inside her mouth. She repositioned herself on the stool, squared her shoulders, took a deep breath.

Just as she was about to unleash her fury, another restaurant patron said to Debra, "Hey, honey. I'm back."

Debra looked up at the milk-chocolate Adonis who stood before her. His gentle eyes mellowed her rage and she relaxed her posture. "Hey." She smiled. "I had your seat, but…." She looked at the rude patron, shrugged.

The unfriendly guy wrapped up his food, grabbed his pop. "Oh, I'm sorry. Here you go." He disappeared into the crowd of carnivores.

Debra lowered her head. "Thank you so much."

"You're more than welcome." He set his carry-out food on the counter.

Debra shifted.

"I'm not staying. I know that you're saving this seat for your girlfriend."

Her eyes measured him.

"I've been watching you since I walked in here." He handed her his business card. "I'm Robert. Call me sometime. I'd like to take you out to dinner."

She averted her eyes away from his, took the business card. "I'm Debra."

"Well, Debra, are you gonna call me?"

She nodded, "Yes, I'll call you."

"All right then. I look forward to talking with you." He left through the front door and waved at Debra as he passed by the window.

She waved.

"Who's that?" Rachel asked as she set her tray on the counter.

"Robert."

"Do I know Robert?"

"I doubt it. I just met him. He kept me from giving a guy a beat down."

"I told you they were awful today." She saw the business card that Debra flipped through her fingers. "So are you going to follow through?"

"Robert might just be what I need to move on from Vincent."

"I'm impressed."

"About?"

"You didn't swallow your tongue when you said 'Vincent'."

"Guess I just needed a little reassurance that I was still fine." She rocked her head, snapped her fingers. "You know how we do."

"Oh, Lord. Let's not get carried away. It's just a man."

"I don't think you saw how fine he was."

"Doesn't matter. He's just a man and you need to proceed with caution." She bit into her crunchy chicken taco. "Ruff."

"Cut your mouth on the taco?"

"No, I'm barking at you to remind you that he's a D-O-G!"

"Whatever, Rachel. I thought you wanted to see me happy."

"I do and you know I do. I want you happy." She raised her brows, said, "*Whole* and happy."

Debra rolled her eyes. "Here, take my new number." She slid a napkin with scribble on it across the counter.

"Oh, so you're in the I-don't-want-him-to-contact-me-as-long-as-he's-in-the-land-of-the-living phase?"

"Yeah, I'm done."

"Uh huh."

"Call me so I can lock you in. I'm tired of giving all of me to a man only to have him play me. Toss me aside like yesterday's trash." She put Rachel's info in her Blackberry. "I'm done making idols of men."

"Men are just dogs. Plain and simple. The sooner you realize that, the better off you'll be."

"Why do I have to accept that men are dogs? They need to change their ways. Grow up."

"You can't get mad at a dog for acting in its nature: peeing on stuff to mark its territory, humping any and everything, salivating for a belly rub." She raised her shoulders. "You know: dog stuff."

"I guess that explains Vincent's behavior, but what about Catherine's betrayal. I thought she was my friend."

"Because you guys had lunch a few times?"

Debra lowered her head.

"What?" Rachel touched Debra's chin with her index finger, lifted her head. "I know you didn't."

"I did."

She tightened her lips. "How many times do I have to tell you that you don't tell women how good your man is in bed?"

"I couldn't help myself. We had just had the best sex ever before I met Catherine for lunch. She noticed my glow and commented on it. Before I knew it, I was telling her all the contortionist positions Vinc—" Remembering the pain made her mouth dry. She swallowed hard, gulped some water, massaged her throat.

"Diarrhea of the mouth."

"She seemed so concerned about our problems." She slapped her hands over her mouth.

"You mean to tell me that you told her about your issues, too?"

Debra nodded.

"You set yourself up for the okey doke, huh?"

"Yeah, I did."

"Nevertheless, that doesn't discount her actions or his for that matter. Wrong is wrong, all day long."

~ ~ ~ ~ ~ ~ ~ ~

When Debra returned to the office, she logged into Facebook. Her investigative tactics had matured so instead of ducking behind trees and telephone poles to follow Vincent, she used the virtual play-by-play diary to stalk him online.

He had uploaded a photo with him and Catherine and changed his status to "in a relationship." Debra scrolled through the posts of romantic banter, until she realized that she had saturated her desk with tears. To avoid being thrust back into the swirling eddy of degradation and despair, she removed Vincent from her friends list. No more Facebook drive-bys. She quit following him on Twitter and deleted his profile from a couple more social networks. She turned off the computer, grabbed her briefcase, left the office.

As she sped down Main Street, she dialed Robert's number. "No sense wasting all of this fineness."

Chapter 6

The Follow-Up Call

Under the tutelage of Doc Reed—a relationship guru whom Sherry met as a recommendation from a friend of a friend—she endured the life-after-Nicholas rights of passage. He helped her cross the burning sands of failed love and rejection to secure a place with the gotta-whole-heart-again sorority.

As the crisis minimized and her strength increased, the need for daily consultations dwindled to sporadic chats. Every week or so, either Sherry called Doc Reed to vent about the devil incarnate—Roxanne—or he called her just to make sure that she hadn't had a relapse.

On this day, after a bout with satan's spawn, Sherry called Doc Reed for a pick-me-up talk.

"Hey, Doc. How are you?"

"Life is good, Sherry. And you?"

"Decent."

"By the way, my accountant thanks you for renewing your sessions."

"I'm sure. You know that I'm a cheapskate—"

"Frugal."

"Okay, frugal, but it is money well spent. I just have a few minutes, so let me bring you up on the latest with Vampira."

"Is she still sucking the life out of you and the rest of the folks at Oracle?"

"She's awful. I told you that her micro-managing and nasty mouth had scared off three employees, right?"

"Yeah."

"Two quit and one retired on disability with a nervous tick by the time she finished with him."

"Wow."

"She even ran off a guy whom I mentored a few years ago when he was still in high school. So the big bosses put me on her because they knew that I could look past her nastiness to get the job done."

"Uh huh."

"Well, before I took the position, I told her that I would give her all that I had to make her look good as long as she treated me with respect."

"Right. As I recall, you gave her two options if she didn't."

"Exactly. I told her that if she came at me like she did those men, then we could handle it one of two ways." Sherry held up her hand, raised a finger with each indictment. "'Woman-to-woman or sister-to-sister; the choice is yours.' Guess how she came at me today."

"Sister-to-sister."

"Yep, that nut came to work bellowing that she wasn't feeling well. I guess the announcement was her way of warning the seven of us in the department to stay clear or suffer her wrath. Anyway, after lunch she yelled at me about not completing an assignment."

"In front of everyone?"

"Oh yeah. She ranted and raved about how incompetent I was and that she couldn't understand how I hadn't been fired a long time ago."

"What did you do?"

"Doc, you would have been proud of me; well initially anyway. I started out using my inside voice; you know, calm, respectful demeanor, but then…."

"What? Then what?"

"The ignoramus stood over me with her finger pointed in my face."

"Not good. Aggressive posturing in an already hostile situation."

"Right. So what do I do?"

"Stand to leverage your posturing."

"Exactly. She's not going to talk down at me while looking down at me. Now for some reason, when I stood, my voice escalated. I was level-headed until she used the 's' word."

"Don't tell me that she called you stupid."

"Dude, when I tell you that I lost it, please believe me. Before the 'id' crossed her lips, I was at warp speed." She paused.

"And?"

"I'm just trying to figure out why that word triggered so much reaction out of me."

"Probably goes back to your angst to be brilliant given your father's comment."

She snapped her fingers. "You are probably right. I bet that's why I bawled like a newborn baby at the women's circle last week, too."

"It's not like you to just haul off and cry. What happened?"

"The first lady called for the women to come together to

encourage and edify one another. I'd say about thirty or so women sat in a circle in the children's sanctuary. We each took turns telling a little about ourselves and one girl talked about how tough her childhood was without her father."

"Your father was present, so why do you think that impacted you so much?"

"I'm getting to that, Doc."

"Oh, my bad. Please continue."

"I'm just piecing this together, geez."

"Okay, okay, continue."

"Anyway, she was a single mother and wanted to go to college, but she didn't see how she'd be able to do it. Between the baby and her money, she was overwhelmed. Well, you know me, Miss Always-Trying-to-Help-Somebody." She paused expecting Doc Reed to comment. "I told her that I'd help her with enrollment, babysitting, tutoring or any other way I could." She paused. "Doc? You still there?"

"Yes, ma'am."

"You're not going to interject your wisdom?"

"Not until you give me the floor. Is it my turn now?"

"Nope. As I offered my help, my throat got scratchy, my words stammered and my eyes poured. I wasn't sobbing, just tears flowing for no apparent reason. I think it was a type of flashback for me. Subconsciously, I saw the flip side of my academic fervor."

"I'd say that your assessment is right on the money. You relived a pain that was triggered by her situation, thus the free flow of emotions."

"I'm getting pretty good at self-diagnosis. I may not need your services for much longer."

"All right young Jedi, you can fool around with Darth Vader if you want to, but you're not ready."

"Anyway back to Rosemary's baby; heads bobbed from behind partitions like the sock-the-gopher game at Dave & Buster's."

"Did you cuss her out?"

"Oh, no. No need for all that. I just told her everything that all the other folks wanted to say but were too afraid to do. By the time I finished blessing out that female, she shrouded herself in a black cloak and withdrew to her desk."

"And the assignment?"

"The dodo bird hadn't checked her email. I had finished it last night before I left work."

"You think she'll apologize?"

"Get serious."

"Given the circumstances you handled yourself well. Good job. Pat yourself on the back."

"Your lips, my hands." Sherry patted her shoulder.

"You have a major life event happening soon with the company closing. How are you adjusting?"

"Outside of Ditzy the Dingbat, I'm doing well."

"And you're following the plan we developed to transition into your new career?"

"Yep. Steady as she goes; full speed ahead."

"Very good; very good. So how's it going with Dwight?"

Almost two years after Nicholas, she released herself to date. A few months later, she met Dwight at the Laundromat two blocks from her apartment. He was new to the city and new to domestic chores. Sherry stopped him just as he started to pour a gallon of bleach onto the rainbow-array of clothes he dumped into the washing machine.

"Ah, so we are moving from life coaching to relationship coaching?"

"Yeah; you couldn't see me, but I switched hats in mid sentence."

She chuckled. "I'm sort of in disbelief at how great this thing is going."

"That's understandable."

"Really?"

"Yeah; you went through a lot with Nicholas—"

"And the brothers who came before him."

"So you may find yourself waiting for something bad to happen."

"I do catch myself anticipating him to stand me up for a date or not call when he promised, but he always comes through. Why am I so quick to expect the worse?"

"Because you aren't used to being in a healthy relationship."

"Tainted heart."

"Wounded. It's your way of staying on guard to protect yourself. Some people even go as far as to sabotage the relationship."

"That's craziness."

"The mind is a powerful thing."

"Speaking of craziness, my girlfriend is in dire straights."

"Debra or Rachel?"

"Guess I've shared my whole life with you, huh?"

"Yep."

"Debra. She just had an awful breakup and she's not adjusting well. If I get her to call, can you help her?"

"But of course. Passion, purpose, prosperity. That's what I do."

"Cool. It's going to take some effort because she's stubborn, opinionated and set in her ways. But I'm not going to quit until she at least talks with you."

"It's pretty serious?"

"Let's just say that if she doesn't get help soon, I'm afraid she's going to do something foolish."

Chapter 7

Tonight's the Night

Debra decided to give herself to Robert. He helped her process through the Vincent matter, relieved her anxiety. They had talked on the phone several times a day over the last four weeks and Skyped when their schedules didn't allow them to meet face-to-face. He shared his dreams and aspirations and encouraged her to do the same. He often alluded to sex, but it was never the topic of conversation. He didn't pressure her like the other men.

"Baby, I'm willing to wait until you're ready. I'm in it for the long haul."

"I appreciate that, Robert. I'm just not trying to take it there."

"I can respect that. How's your day?"

She smiled. "Pretty slow. No court appearances today, so I'm going to work from home. How's your day going?"

"Busy, but good. Just closed a major deal so the guys here at the office are celebrating tonight."

"Oh, are you going with them?"

"Nah, told them that I had other plans."

"You do?"

"Yeah, I'm taking you out for dinner and dancing."

She giggled. "Aw, that's so sweet."

"I know it's only our third date, but it seems like I've known you all of my life. You're easy to talk to and we have a great time toget—"

The phone went silent for a few seconds.

"Robert? You still there?"

Silence.

"Robert?" She checked her cell phone to make sure that the call had not been dropped.

He came back on the line. "Sorry about that. That was my boss trying to convince me to join them."

"You having second thoughts?"

"Are you kidding? Those guys don't hold a candle to you. Be ready at seven and wear something extra special. I'm taking you to the Sidebar in the Oregon District."

"I'm excited. See you soon."

"Bye, baby."

"Bye." She kissed into the air, lingered there for a moment before hanging up the phone. She looked at the clock. "Oh, Lord. It's almost twelve o'clock."

Debra leapt out of her replacement queen-sized bed. Several of the decorative pillows fell to the floor. She had much to do in preparation for the big night and the timing couldn't have been better. She had gotten a mani-pedi the day before and already had a hair appointment scheduled.

She took a quick shower, threw on a sweat suit and then darted off to the salon. She arrived at Treneis Hair Studio just as her stylist, Annette, was finishing with a client.

Annette said, "Hey, give me two minutes to clean up and I'll be right with you."

"Okey dokey."

A few minutes later, she called Debra to her station. "So what'll it be for you today, Dee?"

"Got a hot date tonight, so I need the works."

"Is this the same guy you told me about the last time you were here?"

"Yeah, it is."

"Wow, he's sticking around."

"I know. He's really a great guy. He impressed me from day one with his quick wit and charm. And talk about conversation. We never run out of things to say. It's effortless to be with him."

"I'm jealous."

"Girl, don't be jealous. Your guy is coming."

"I'm not asking for much: a job, a car and his own place."

They laughed.

"Well, Robert has all that *and* good looks. And he always smells so wonderful." She closed her eyes to admire his masculine scent.

"Hello? Earth to Dee."

"Oh, sorry. Got caught up."

"Yeah you did." Annette feathered her fingers through Debra's hair. "It's relaxer time."

"Yeah, I know."

"You want it trimmed?"

"How about giving me something short and sassy? I have a new man, I want a new look."

"You sure? 'Cause once I whack you can't go back."

"I'm sure."

"You are doing a lot to impress this guy." She fanned the cape, placed it around Debra. "Something you want to tell me?"

She looked in the mirror at her stylist's reflection. "Tonight's the night."

Annette raised her brows. "The night for what?"

"You know: it."

"You guys haven't had sex yet?"

"Uh, no. I'm not a first-date freak."

"Oh, well excuse me, Miss Prim and Proper."

"Now see, don't even go there."

"I'm just saying, you old highfalutin' thang."

"Whatever. He's a great guy; so considerate and thoughtful. If I reach for the car-door handle, he frowns and tells me, 'I got you.'"

"Get out of here."

"I know, right? Chivalry is not dead."

She raised her hand to high-five with Annette. The ladies laughed.

"He deserves to have me. It'll be my way of congratulating him for doing well at work."

"Uh huh."

"Get to cutting. I need my eyebrows and mustache waxed. Oh yeah, can you trim my sideburns too?"

~ ~ ~ ~ ~ ~ ~

Debra arrived home about half past four. She ran into the master bathroom, lit a candle and flipped on the radio. She disrobed, touched up her heels with a pumice stone and then slid into the lavender-scented bubble bath as *Chocolate Legs* by Eric Benét played.

She exhaled, soaked for a moment and then initiated her pre-relations ritual. She lathered her body five times with Dove and then shaved her underarms, legs and southern bell. She used foot scrub on her feet, palms and elbows followed by a loofah full of warm-vanilla-sugar body wash. She wanted every inch of her body to whisper "soft to the touch." She patted herself dry so as not to leave whelps on her flawless, but sensitive skin and then headed for the walk-in closet.

"What to wear? What to wear?" She perused the

expansive wardrobe for several minutes, grabbed outfits, held them up to her. She twisted from side to side as she looked in the full-length mirror affixed to the wall before settling for a form-fitted black dress and four-inch stilettos.

Debra stepped out of the closet, with outfit in hand, checked the clock radio. "Ten minutes to six!" She rummaged through her unmentionables drawer for the bright-red lace bra and panty set. She didn't expect Robert to notice that the lingerie matched the soles of her shoes.

She splashed on a variety of Bath and Body Works scents to create a unique aroma, slipped the dress over her head, careful not to mess up her new 'do. With great precision, she painted on the Mac makeup and then squirted Angel on her wrists and neck.

With ten minutes to spare, she packed a few toiletries, a wrap scarf and a change of clothes into a small bag. She headed down the hall, but then went back to her room to grab her after-five purse. Just as she walked into the living room, the doorbell rang. She put the purse and overnight bag on the coffee table.

"He is so punctual." She shimmied to shake off the sexual urges, adjusted her dress, opened the door.

"Wow, you look beautiful." He pulled her close, lifted her off her feet, gave her a sensual kiss. "I missed you so much."

She whispered, "I missed you, too," as she ran her hands down his well-defined chest.

"Let me see all of you." He took her by the hand and spun her around. "I like it like that."

She giggled, went to twirl her hair, but the shortened locks were out of reach. "How do you like my hair?"

"It's nice, real nice." He handed her a bouquet of pink and white roses arrayed with baby's breath.

She squealed. "Oh, they are beautiful. My first bouquet."

She breathed in the sweet aroma of the field of flowers.

"I gave you one for every day we've known each other."

"Twenty-eight roses?"

"I'm not the traditional kind of guy."

Her heart fluttered. "And I like that in you." She tiptoed to kiss him on the cheek.

"All right, now. I'm trying to be a gentleman." He kissed her forehead. "We need to get going. We have reservations for seven-thirty."

"Let's go." She stepped toward the door, spoke over her shoulder. "Can you grab my bags on the table?"

Robert walked to the table, picked up the bags. "I get the purse, but what's the other bag?"

She blushed, bowed her head, turned on the porch light. "It's my overnight bag."

He smiled like the Cheshire cat from *Alice in Wonderland*. "Oh, so I get to see the 'Ms. Dee' tattoo, huh?"

"If you act right." She giggled.

~ ~ ~ ~ ~ ~ ~ ~

Per his usual attentiveness, Robert opened doors for Debra, escorted her to the passenger side of the car, assisted her with her chair. A true gentleman. Their conversation was light, intriguing and somewhat seductive.

When they arrived at his apartment, he offered her a seat on the black leather couch. He disappeared into the kitchen and returned with two glasses of champagne.

"For the lady." He handed Debra a glass.

"Why thank you, kind sir." She ran the tip of her tongue along the rim of the fluted glass.

As Debra took dainty sips, Robert finished his drink and then knelt on the floor. He slid off her shoes, massaged her feet, licked her toes. She quivered. Although Robert was not her first, Debra was nervous. She only gave herself to men with whom she saw a future and his touch flooded her with memories of failed relationships.

He noticed the tension in her body, whispered, "It's okay." He caressed her hands, stroked her face, kissed the tattoo on her inner thigh. He stood, picked her up, carried her to his bedroom.

She resolved her apprehension by affirming, *He's the one. He's the one.* His gentleness and passion excited her during their intimate bliss.

As they lay in bed, his arms holding her tightly, Debra thought, *I can do this forever.* A full smile washed across her face. She looked up at Robert, in a sultry voice she said, "I'm so glad you're in my l—"

The Maxwell ringtone—*Pretty Wings*—interrupted her.

Robert sat up, turned to the nightstand.

"Just let it go to voicemail, baby."

"Can't do that," he said, as he reached for the phone. "Yeah, this Rob."

Debra huffed.

Robert got out of bed.

"Where are you going?"

He held up his index finger to silence her and then walked into the bathroom.

Debra sat up, crossed her arms over her perky bosom.

Five minutes later, he returned. "I hate to do this to you, but I have to go."

"Go?"

"Yeah, that was my boss. Guess I didn't have a choice after all. I have to show my face at the celebration."

"Oh, okay. Well, give me a few minutes to freshen up and I'll be ready." She jumped out of bed, walked toward the bathroom.

"Babe, you won't be able to join me on this one. It's just

the guys. You wouldn't have a good time anyway."

"Any time with you is a good time. Besides, I really want to meet the co-workers you're always talking about."

"Yeah, I know, babe, but there'll be other times."

Debra stopped, looked Robert in the eyes. "Are you trying to get rid of me?"

"It's not like that. I have responsibilities at work; that's all. Don't read anything extra into it."

She sulked, pouted. "I was so looking forward to cooking you breakfast in the morning after another round or two or three of lovemaking."

"Do you take rain checks?" He kissed her on the forehead.

She smiled.

Except for the R & B tunes that played on WROU, the ride to her house was quiet. When Robert pulled up in the driveway, Debra waited for him to open the passenger-side door.

"Come on, babe. I'm already late."

He leaned toward her. She closed her eyes, prepared for a kiss. He reached past her and opened the door.

With slow, intentional movements, she stepped out of the car, grabbed the overnight bag from the backseat.

With his hands on the steering wheel, Robert looked out of the windshield. "I need you to pick up the pace."

"I'm sorry. When can I see you again?"

He reached for the door. "I'll call you." He closed the door and then sped off. The breeze from the passing car whipped under her dress.

Debra's walk to the front door was like trekking through wet cement. The lit porch that was supposed to deter unwanted guests was a beacon that taunted her early arrival. She rationalized that her heaviness was from a hard work week.

Inside, she kicked off her stilettos, dropped the bag and shuffled to the bedroom. She plopped on the bed and cried herself to sleep.

~ ~ ~ ~ ~ ~ ~

The next morning, Debra crawled out of bed. She tossed the black dress in the dry-clean-only hamper, put on an oversized sweat suit. She washed the remaining glitter liner and eye shadow from her face, brushed her teeth, combed and wrapped her hair.

She looked in the mirror. "I will not revert to my old ways. New day; new me." The declaration lasted all of an hour before she called Robert.

His voicemail greeting started. "Hey, This is Rob. You know what to do."

In a cheerful tone, she said, "Hey, baby. I had a great time last night. Call me when you get in. I want to know how the celebration went and since we couldn't do breakfast, I want to cook you dinner."

She busied herself cleaning the stove and wiping down the kitchen cabinets. By two o'clock, she hadn't heard from him. She called and got voicemail after two rings.

"Hey, Rob. I'm sure you're busy working, but call me so I know you got in okay."

She scrubbed the Jacuzzi, two toilets and a vanity. She used an old toothbrush to remove mold growing in the grout of the tiled shower. She wiped the sweat on her forehead with the back of her hand, called Robert. The call went straight to voicemail. "Robert, I'm starting to feel a little played so call me."

She vacuumed the area rugs, mopped the kitchen floor, organized the pantry. She jiggled the cord between the phone and the wall jack, lifted the receiver, checked to make sure it had a dial tone. It did.

At ten o'clock, Debra hopped in the shower to wash away the dust, sweat and disappointment and then she climbed into bed. Before she turned off the lamp on the nightstand, she made one last call. Voicemail.

"You're just like all the others! You no-good dog!" She slammed the phone on the receiver.

Chapter 8

Cleaning House

Before the sun peered through the darkness, Debra was up cleaning. A couple hours into her I-have-to-redirect-my-attention-so-that-I-don't-do-something-stupid crusade, she called her pick-me-up crew.

"Good morning, R. J. Nance Marketing. This is Sylvia. How may I help you?"

"Hey, Sylvia. Is Rachel available?"

"Good morning, Ms. Hampton. Ms. Nance is meeting with a client. She should be done in a few minutes. Would you like her voicemail or should I have her call you?"

"Have her call me. Thanks."

She hung up, walked toward the kitchen when the phone rang. Debra raced back to the phone, grabbed the receiver, checked the caller ID. With a rattle of disappointment, she said, "Oh, hi, Sherry."

"Wow and good morning to you, too."

"I'm sorry. I just thought you were somebody else."

"Well, if I still wore my esteem on my shoulder, I'd be hurt. But since I'm no longer that woman, what's going on with you? How'd it go with Robert?"

"Awful."

"What happened? The sex was pathetic?"

"No, the sex was great," she sighed, propped the phone between the crook of her neck and right shoulder, grabbed the feather duster and Pledge.

"So?"

"Promise you won't say I told you so."

"I promise." Sherry bit her lip, covered her mouth with her hand for extra security.

"He took me home right after and I haven't heard from him since." After a significant pause, she continued. "Go ahead. Let me have it."

"Why didn't you call me sooner?"

"I was too hurt. You would've gotten a lot of cussing and crying."

"If that's what you need, then that's what I'm here for."

"Nah, incoherent babble won't do. I need to talk through this one. I really thought that he—"

The call-waiting tone interrupted her.

"Hold on a second, Sherry. This might be him." She clicked to the other line. "Hello?"

"Hola, señorita. Como esta?"

"Hey, Rachel."

"You've been cleaning haven't you?"

"How'd you know?"

"Well for one, you didn't reply to my greeting in your usual 'muy bien.' And when you didn't leave a message of elation with Sylvia, I knew something wasn't right. Still depending on the power of Pine Sol to make you feel better, huh?"

"You know me well."

"You're looking like Aunt Jemima, too, aren't you?"

"Uh, if you're referring to my cleaning attire, then that

would be a yes." She snapped her fingers. "Oh, shoot. I forgot I have Sherry on the other line. Hang up and I'll call you back on three-way."

"Okey dokey. Call my direct number."

Debra clicked back to the original call. "Sherry, you still there?"

"Yep. Was it him?"

"No; Rachel. Can you call her direct line? I always drop the call when I try to do this three-way thingy on my house phone."

With the crew on the phone, the venting session ensued.

Debra said, "What is it about men that makes them think it's okay to love us and then leave us?" She sprayed furniture polish on the cherry-wood armoire.

Sherry said, "They can only do to us what we allow."

"Look Ms. I-am-satisfied-with-my-current-dating-situation, I'm not trying to hear your philosophical soliloquy. I'm not talking about what we do; I'm talking about what they do."

"But that's the whole thing. They respond to us."

Rachel said, "Oh, Lord. Here comes her spiel about her success with the relationship coach."

"See, neither of you is open to change. Only a crazy man keeps doing the same thing and expects different results."

"Actually we have made some changes," Debra said, as she used an old T-shirt on a stubborn water spot. "Remember how we used to handle this type of situation?"

The trio chorused, "Stake out!" They laughed.

"Why in the world did we think that hiding in the bushes was going to make that man want us?" Sherry asked.

Rachel said, "It was my way to validate suspicions of his cheating."

Debra dropped the phone, picked it up again. "Sorry

about that. Juggling too much. My logic was if I caught him with another woman, I could mess things up for him."

"And what value is in that? Did it change his attraction toward you?"

"Look, Sherry, just because you're in a happy place now don't act like we didn't do some drive-bys on your behalf."

"And I'm embarrassed about it. You mentioned 'logic' earlier. There's no logic in squatting in foliage at night. Remember the time you got poison ivy? Took tons of calamine lotion and a shot to clear it up."

Debra dusted the stained-wood floor boards. "Whatever."

"Dressed up like cat burglars with flashlights. And—"

"I looked good in my skin-tight jumpsuit."

"And a flask of coffee. What kind of mess? Beautiful, intelligent women, earning good money and full of insecurity. Hold on." Inaudible words seeped through the muffled receiver. Sherry returned to the conversation at a church-mouse volume, "Hey, let me put you on hold for a minute." She muted the line.

Rachel said, "Whew, saved by the boss."

They chuckled.

"Rachel, I'm thirty-five years old and still going through the same mess with men. I know there's got to be someone out there who will treat me like a lady."

"And be employed. We cannot forget employed."

"Yeah, but at this point, I'd settle for actively seeking employment."

"Don't settle. You'll end up regretting it. Use me as an example. I'd rather be pushing forty and single, than pushing forty and miserable in marriage."

"Wait just a minute. You're pushing forty; I'm thirty-five."

"Are your hormones in hyper drive?"

"You already know my southern bell has been screaming at me all year long."

"Right, little spasms that tell you, 'Hey, I'm down here. Don't forget about me.'"

"She has definitely made her presence known." She looked at her southern bell, placed her index finger to her mouth. "Shhhh. Cut out all that noise."

"Are you stressing about getting married? Having kids?"

"Uh, yeah. Thus this conversation." Debra filled a bucket with warm water and Pine Sol.

"Then you, my dear sister, are pushing forty. Color it up however you like, but the tick tock of your biological clock has you tripping."

"Ticking brings tripping, huh?"

"Yep. Your esteem takes a lickin' and your ovaries keep on tickin'."

"Okay, get out of my uterus. Why are you experiencing spasms, Rachel? You have access to unlimited sex."

Sherry came back on the line. "Sorry about that. Roxanne is on a rampage today. Now where was I?"

"I just asked Rachel about her sex life."

Sherry said, "Rachel, how's it going with Brian?"

"We are not about to change this to the Rachel and Brian Show. This session is for Ms. Dee."

Debra said, "It most definitely is." She soaked a sponge mop in the solution, squeezed out the excess liquid, cleaned the hardwood floors.

"I'm just asking if you guys have worked through the marital woes."

"No and I don't know that we ever will. He hurt me deep and until I can get past that, I can't free my heart to forgive him."

"I'm surprised that your logical side can't override your

emotional side," she gestured Spock's Vulcan hand wave. "Ms. Live-Long-and-Prosper."

"You know how I do; tuck it away so that I can keep moving forward. It's not so much the incident with his brother as it is years of feeling like I wasn't his priority."

"You need to break down those walls."

"Walls? Girl, I have built a skyscraper and taken residence in the penthouse. He's begged and pleaded for my forgiveness, but I don't know how to let this go. If I could, I would. I'm stressed to the max. Got a bald spot behind my left ear and my temples are thinning. It's causing me all kinds of issues: physical and emotional."

"And spiritual."

"I'm not going there today, oh holy one."

Debra cleared her throat. "Uh, excuse me, but I initiated this powwow. Bring it back in to Ms. Dee, would you please?"

"You're right. Sorry about that," Sherry said. "I know I might get slapped for saying this, but why even have sex, if you know you aren't supposed to be giving it up until you're married?"

"I know, but I thought he was the one."

"I don't see why that makes a difference."

"It doesn't. At this point, I'm just hoping that God will grade me on a curve since I waited a month."

"You are a hot mess."

Rachel chimed in. "So what are you going to do to take back control?"

"How do you mean?"

"He's one up on you now that you made umpteen hysterical calls to him. He knows you're desperate."

"Keep talking." She switched the phone to her left ear.

"We have to get you back in the driver's seat. Make him

spin out of control. Do some—"

Sherry interjected, "Vengeance is mine saith the Lord. I will repay."

Debra and Rachel said, "Shut up, Sherry!"

"Fine. If you don't want to listen to the voice of reason, I'm going into stealth mode. Have fun on your self-destruct mission." She muted the call.

"Good riddance," Rachel said. "He's up to something. You two were going strong for weeks and then all of a sudden the day after you have sex; nothing. He's got to have another woman."

"That's what I'm thinking. I just need to know," Debra said, as she plopped on the couch exhausted. She sighed. "Maybe I'll show up on his job and act a complete fool."

Sherry came back on the line. "And who will look the fool? Him or you?" She muted again.

"How about I bust a window in his car or slash his tires?"

Sherry un-muted. "Seen enough *Judge Judy* to know that you won't get away with that one. Then the whole world will see how desperate you are to got a man " She pressed the mute button.

"Okay, how about I pay a detective to follow him? That's subtle."

Un-mute. "Subtly stupid and a waste of money." Mute.

"That's so aggravating. Sherry, get back on the line!"

Un-mute. "When a man really wants something, there's nothing that anyone can do to keep him from it. If you hear from him, he's into you. If you don't, then I hate to say it, but he got what he wanted and he's done with you."

"That's so unfair."

"Men are how they are."

Rachel curled the corner of her lip. "You act like you just know men so well."

"No, it's not that I know men, but I am resourceful."

"Resourceful?"

"Yeah, when I don't know something, I hire someone who does."

"Well, I don't know if Robert has another woman, so I'm going to hire a detective."

"Not the same thing, sweetie. Nice try though. Were you even in a committed, monogamous relationship with Robert when you gave up the goody goo-goo?"

"Oh, God, she's talking *Hitch* again," Rachel said.

"Sarcasm is not going to get her through this, but my relationship coach definitely can. I haven't stooped to those grade-school tactics and things are going great for me."

Rachel said, "If your coach is so great at matchmaking, then why haven't we met this wonderful new man?"

"It's not so much the man—who by the way is named Dwight—it's about my perspective on relationships in general." Sherry smiled. "I'm taking it nice and slow with Dwight. Once he's proven himself, then I'll let you two meet him."

"He's a figment of your imagination, conjured up to deal with the pain of lost love. You're living in a fantasy world."

"Rachel, are you serious? Dwight is not someone I pulled out of a hat. He's real, tangible and amazing. I'm just following the doc's prescription to make sure that he is what I need him to be."

Debra said, "Okay, Sherry, I give. How do I get in touch with Hitch?"

"His name is John Reed, Junior, but I call him Doc Reed."

Debra stood, paced the sparkling floor. "Doc? I'm not talking to a shrink. There is nothing wrong with my mental capacity. I am not insane, just a little relationship challenged. I'm not about to stretch out on a plastic couch and talk to a complete stranger referred by the goddess of love. You think I'm suicidal or something?"

"Come on, Dee."

"Only cuckoos chat with psychiatrists. I am not in that line. Next!"

"He's not a doctor. He's experienced in relationship dynamics and he helps heal broken hearts. Give him a chance."

"So what's his fee?"

"Now he's not cheap, but he's worth every penny. His insight changed my life."

"So he's not a doctor, but he charges like one. Interesting."

"Just call him. He's a great listener and full of manly advice. Besides, if you don't do something soon, we're going to find you in a corner spit-shining shoes."

Chapter 9

Relationship 101

Debra arrived at North River Coffee House early to get her favorite seat: the bistro-style table for two that faced the large picture window. She walked to the counter and greeted Angela, the restaurant manager.

"Hey, Angela. How was your weekend?"

"Pretty good. Haven't seen you in awhile. How've you been?"

"I don't want to talk about it."

"Oh, it's like that?"

"Yep. Awful."

"Well, how about we start this week off right? The usual?"

Debra smiled. "Yeah, but just the chai tea for now. I'll be ready for lunch in a little bit."

"Extra-hot chai tea, hold the foam. Coming right up."

"Thanks." Debra took a seat, admired the pictures and wall-mounted displays from local artists. She bopped to the urban beat that piped through the speakers: audible but not overbearing. "Listening to *Special Friend* by *Tonya Baker* again, huh?"

"You know it." Angela said, as she placed the tea in front of Debra.

"Thank you much, ma'am."

"You are more than welcome."

Debra watched the steam dance on the top of the cup. Her leg bounced without restraint under the table. She massaged her temples and then preened her hair. She called Sherry.

"Girl, I'm not too sure about this."

"What are you afraid of?"

"Talking to a complete stranger about my love life."

"You mean the lack thereof."

"Ha! You are so funny. Anyway, I don't know him like that. I can't open up about all the mess these men have put me through. He's a man."

"Right. How better to learn about men than from a man? It just makes sense."

"I guess."

"He's helped me rethink my actions and reactions to men. And look at me now."

"I can hear you beaming through the phone. Okay, I'll give it a try."

"That's all I ask. If it doesn't work for you, then you haven't lost anything."

"What does he get out of this?"

"He genuinely loves relationships. The dynamics between men and women; the rules of engagement; the whole song and dance. Kind of like how you love torts and contracts. It just makes him tick."

"Gotcha." She noticed an unfamiliar patron walk into the coffee house. "Is he caramel brown with wavy salt and pepper hair?"

"Yep."

"Okay, he just walked in. Talk at you later."

"Smooches."

"Smooches." Debra waved over the man, extended her hand. "Hi, are you Doc Reed?"

He nodded, shook her hand. "Yes. It's a pleasure to meet you, Debra."

"Same here."

"You know I'm a relationship coach and not a doctor, right?"

"Yeah, that's just how Sherry referred to you and the name kind of stuck. Do you want to order lunch first?"

"Sure."

Debra stood, walked toward the counter. She introduced Doc Reed to Angela and then placed her order.

Reading the menu board, Doc Reed asked, "So what do you recommend?"

"Everything here is scrumptious. Soups, salads, sandwiches and some of the best desserts. That one there," she pointed to the chocolate-turtle dessert made by The Wright Cheesecake, "is of the devil." She smacked her lips, turned to Angela. "I don't care what I say; I cannot have a slice today."

Angela smiled.

Doc Reed said, "I'll have the chicken gumbo soup and turkey sandwich."

"Excellent choice. That's what I'm having."

Angela said, "Debra, do you want toasted wheat bread and American cheese?"

"Yes, ma'am. As always."

Doc Reed turned to Debra. "So you're a creature of habit, huh?"

"Pretty much."

They returned to the table. Debra looked around the room, fidgeted in her seat, wiped the table for imaginary food remnants.

Noticing her apprehension, Doc Reed initiated the conversation. "I hear you have some exciting things going on in your relationships."

"Exciting is not how I would describe it."

"Yeah, Sherry told me."

She leaned back in the chair, folded her arms. "What else did she tell you?"

"She can relate to your struggles because she's done the same things."

Debra looked up and to the left.

"Not to worry. Our conversations are confidential. Sherry will only know what you tell her."

"Really?"

"That's the only way you'll feel free to share everything with me. I'm not here to judge you and I'm not going to tell anyone what you tell me."

"Cool. I'm still not comfortable with this arrangement, but I am open to listening."

"That's fair. Let the teaching begin." He cleared his throat. "A man will tell you everything you want to hear to draw you in. Once he gets it, all that long suffering skeets out of his body."

"'It' being sex?"

"Yes. Let me give you a snapshot into the mind of a man."

Debra leaned forward, propped her chin on her hand.

"Initially, a man sees a woman as a walking vagina."

Debra furrowed her brow, sat back in the chair. "Excuse me?"

"A walking vagina."

"I take offense to that." She crossed her arms, pursed her lips and rolled her eyes.

"I'm telling you how a man thinks. If you'd rather, we can refer to it as a pocketbook, funky box. How about the goody box?" He nodded, satisfied with the analogy. "I'm going to step you through the forbidden secrets of the goody box."

"Do men really think of us like that? I mean I know they're visually stimulated, but a walking va— a walking goody box? Amazing." She grabbed a pen from her purse and used a napkin as a writing pad.

"Exactly. It is amazing." He gazed off into the middle distant and then looked at Debra. "It's a precious commodity that women often give away without much thought, then wonder why men are so quick to leave after getting it."

Debra released an extended sigh. "I know about that." She shook her head. "I really thought Robert was into me."

"Why did you think that?"

"He told me; he showed me. But when I called him after, he didn't answer."

"I hate to tell you this, but after he hit it, he probably sent your calls to voicemail."

"You think?"

"I can almost guarantee it. Believe me when I tell you that a man can hold his breath for about three months."

"Hold his breath?"

"He can say and do all the right stuff for about three months in his quest for the goody box."

"Are you serious?"

The restaurant manager placed a tray of food on the table. "Do you need anything else?"

Debra smiled. "We're good. Thanks, Angela."

Doc Reed inhaled. "Smells delicious."

"It is," Debra said, as she bit into the grilled turkey sandwich with caramelized onions. "They take good care of me here." She dabbed at the warm cheese in the corner of her mouth. "Now back to the goody box."

"When a man first meets a woman he processes from his eyes, to his crotch, to his heart. His emotional, spiritual and mental maturity will determine whether he will allow that attraction to become more than visual. You can be talking about quantum physics, but in his mind he's thinking, 'Lord have mercy. I can't wait to toss up that big, brown—'"

"Dogs."

"Wait a minute now. Just because a man is wired for physical attraction doesn't make him a dog."

"I beg to differ."

"We are emotional beings, too. It just takes us longer to get there."

"You're telling me that men get emotionally vested?"

"Yep. The heart gets involved, but only after a period of time."

She took a sip of chai tea. "I have yet to experience that."

"That's because you don't give it enough time."

"Are you trying to say that I'm an easy win?"

"I'm not being judgmental, just stating what I know. The goody box has a built-in power source. It's like a magnetic field that draws men toward it. If your desire is to take that attraction from the groin to the heart, you have to withhold it. It's the only way to get him emotionally connected to you."

"This is just too much. It goes against everything I know about men. If he loves sex and I give him sex, then logic says that he will love me."

"Doesn't work that way."

Debra threw her hands up as if to surrender and then dropped them on the table.

In a sing-song voice, Doc Reed said, "Now don't be overwhelmed," he patted her hands and then continued, "because I'm with you. And if you'll allow me, we're going to work through your emotional component."

"There's nothing wrong with my emotions. I am not emotional!" She put her hand on her hip, stared at Doc Reed.

He chuckled. "You're right. There is nothing wrong with your emotions, but if you lead with your heart and he leads with logic, it's like trying to dance the waltz with two lead partners. A hot mess. You fall all over each other; step on each other's feet. Get what I'm saying?"

Debra nodded.

"You get involved with a guy. He says the right things, takes you on a couple of dates, makes you feel like you're the only one for him. Even if he never verbalizes it, your heart and mind convince you otherwise."

Debra blushed. "How do you know that?"

He smiled. "And after a couple of weeks, you're smitten. You respond out of emotion whereas he works from logic."

"Okay, okay. I'm understanding."

"Your challenge is to not fall into the knee-jerk reactions that follow emotions."

"I'm confused again."

"Whatever you would normally do in your dealings with men, don't do it. It hasn't worked for you up to this point and it won't work for you in the future." He paused. "You know; the meaning of insanity?"

"Yeah, yeah, yeah. Sherry is definitely your student. So what knee-jerk thing should I not do?" She rocked her head, sucked her teeth.

"Let's start with an easy one. Don't call him."

"Don't call him?"

"Yeah, am I speaking Swahili? Let him make the first move. Can you do that?"

"Oh, now you're going to be sarcastic."

"No, really I'm not. The process of reprogramming your response will take practice and time. I'm trying to create awareness for you so that when a situation arises, you know how to respond. As quiet as it's kept, men are not complicated."

"Whatever."

"We're not. It all goes back to the emotion versus logic approach. If you want to catch a man's undivided attention, you have to know how he thinks."

"Don't call?"

"Don't call. If he's a dog, make him beg." He rubbed his hands together to clear away the bread crumbs. "Want to know how to avoid the heartaches of your past?"

She expelled a puff of air. "Duh, yeah."

"Know what you want before you get emotionally connected. Because once your emotions kick in, everything gets fuzzy and blurry. You don't make rational decisions and you compromise."

She shrugged. "It sounds easy enough, but I'm not convinced."

"Not convinced, hmm. What do you want out of a relationship?"

"I want to be happy."

"Okay, well let's narrow that down some. What makes you happy? Is it just being in the relationship or do you expect more?"

"Well of course I want more."

"Then that's what you need to capture. Work on a list of specific must-haves and preferences. No generalizations or vague descriptions."

"Give me a couple of examples."

"Instead of saying that you want to be happy, how about you want to receive a bouquet of roses every Monday?"

She crinkled her nose. "I'm not into roses, but I get what you mean."

"Or let's say that you want a man who loves God."

"And I do."

"Okay, does that mean he attends church weekly or just major holidays? Is he actively involved in several ministries or just acknowledges that a superior being exists?"

She nodded.

"For everything you write, note why it's important to you, then classify it as an absolute necessity—the deal breaker— or something you'd just like to have."

"Kind of like job descriptions. They require a bachelor's degree, but a master's is preferred."

"Right. You can get the job with a four-year degree, but your chances are better with more education. Once you finish the list, we'll use it as a road map to guide you through the next relationship."

Debra scribbled a couple more notes on the napkin. "I have to be honest; I didn't want to talk to you."

"Yeah, I know. Most chocolate people don't like counselors. For some reason, they think it certifies them as crazy."

Debra smirked and then raised her hand.

He chuckled. "Everyone needs to talk to someone to get through their problems. You're no different."

"If you say so."

"Not to worry, we'll get through this and you'll be all right."

Chapter 10

Human Resources

Rachel was glad to have Conrad Bateman on her team as office manager. His loyalty to her firm—a godsend—minimized the effect of Bob's mutiny. Conrad's unassuming demeanor allowed him to meld into the environment like a fixture on the wall. The nonthreatening posturing was perceived as insignificant and thus made him privy to bits of the takeover which he shared with Rachel

Conrad's gait caused excessive wear on the heels of his shoes which he frequently replaced with Goodwill throwbacks. He was about as tall as Batman's Boy Wonder and for the last two years, he used the vision insurance offered through RJ Nance Marketing to replace the lenses in his Clark Kent frames. Although he was a groomed man, he would never be a spokesperson for Proactiv.

Rachel buzzed Sylvia on the intercom.

"Sylvia, have Conrad come in here please."

"Yes, Ms. Nance."

Two minutes later, Conrad knocked on the door.

"Come in."

Conrad entered the room, left the door open. "Good morning, Ms. Nance. How are you today?" He stood in front of Rachel's desk.

"I'm well, thanks." She pointed to the chair. "Take a seat and let's get started."

Conrad sat on the edge of the chair, readied his pen and steno pad.

Rachel steepled her index fingers, stood, paced the office. Walking helped her collect her thoughts; a ritual that could take up to twenty minutes.

Conrad remained silent as he watched her walk from one end of the large office to the other.

Rachel sat at her desk and then searched through a stack of folders. "Now where is that file on Carrington Corp?"

"Here it is." Conrad handed her a manila folder.

"How did you know that was next on my agenda?"

"It's my job to know what you need before you do."

"Clairvoyant, are we?"

"No, just tuned in to what needs to be done to keep your company efficient and flourishing."

"Hiring you was the smartest thing I've done in awhile." She smiled. "I know I've said it a thousand times, but thanks again for thwarting Bob's attempts to steal all of my clients."

"Again, you're welcome. If I had been a little more assertive, maybe he wouldn't have caused the damage he did."

"Are you kidding me? Your efforts kept him from destroying everything I built. The collateral damage is minimal when I think of what could have happened."

"I admire what you've created and couldn't sit back with a do-nothing attitude. You're good people and deserve better than that." He paused, adjusted his watch. "I'm committed to helping you reach your business objectives."

"That's good to know."

"I find your intelligence and power attractive qualities,"

Conrad said, as he slid his glasses up the bridge of his nose. "Not many women can pull off both and still maintain their femininity."

"Thanks, Conrad. It's great to be appreciated." Rachel read over the documents.

"Your husband is a lucky man."

Without looking up, she said, "If you say so."

"You don't agree?"

Before she could reply, Sylvia interrupted on the intercom.

"Ms. Nance, your husband is on line one."

"Thanks." She looked at Conrad. "Give me just one minute."

He nodded.

In her corporate voice, she said, "Yeah, babe. What's up?" A few seconds into the conversation, Rachel rolled her eyes and let her gaze linger at the ceiling. "Brian, why are you asking me where *your* kids are?" After a reserved tongue lashing, she slammed the phone on the receiver. "Sorry about that."

"No problem."

"I don't like handling personal matters on company time, but some things just can't be avoided."

"I'm sure it's not easy to manage home and work, yet you seem to do it so effortlessly. A modern-day Super Woman."

"Ha! Not quite."

"Okay, Wonder Woman then. You have stamina, agility, the ability to discern the truth—"

"Yeah, with my magic lasso." Rachel pulled the retractable ID badge and let it snap back.

"And you definitely look like an Amazonian goddess."

Rachel looked at him from the corner of her eyes.

"I don't mean to be disrespectful. I'm truly impressed by you." He cleared his throat. "As for keeping up with the kids' schedules, how about using a dry-erase board? You can post it on the refrigerator."

"Actually, I have one, but never find the time to fill in the details."

"Make it an activity with you and the kids. While you're cooking dinner, they can make color-coded magnets for their various activities."

"I am not the artsy-craftsy one, but I like the concept."

"Kill three birds with one stone: populate the calendar, cook dinner and spend quality time with your precious babies."

"I love how you think."

Chapter 11

The Making of Mr. Right

Anxious to start on her list, Debra left the eatery on Salem Avenue and headed downtown to Rachel's office. Her friend of almost twenty years had built her agency into a tiny empire with a thousand dollars, long hours and discipline.

She employed about fifteen people, including Sylvia, the first to appear when the elevator door opened on the seventh floor.

"Good afternoon, Ms. Hampton. How are you today?"

"I'm well, Sylvia. How about yourself?"

"Staying busy. You know how Ms. Nance is." She nodded toward Rachel's office, lowered her voice. "She's in there giving someone a good chewing out right now. She'll be with you in a moment. Would you like a cup of coffee while you wait?"

"No, thanks." Debra walked to the waiting area, grabbed copies of *Above Rubies* and *JO* magazines, sat on the plush chair. She admired Rachel's flair for decorating. The warm earth tones were soothing and inviting. Everything about the office indicated classy, stylish. From lighting to wall hangings to trash receptacles, the atmosphere created a sense of prestige.

Sylvia approached Debra. "Ms. Nance will see you now."

"Thanks, Sylvia." Debra followed her to the office. Not that she didn't know the way, but Sylvia was committed to her executive-secretary duties and treated all visitors like million-dollar clients.

Sylvia opened the door. "Ms. Nance, your next appointment is here."

Rachel stood from behind the desk. Her slender frame complemented the St. John skirt suit that hit a few inches above her knees. Shoulder-length hair framed her tiny, round face, which was speckled with a few freckles on her nose. "Thank you."

Debra entered the office, Sylvia closed the door.

In a melodious tone, Debra said, "What's up, Rachel Jean?"

"Hey, Ms. Dee. How are you?" They greeted each other with a hug. "You had your meeting with Doc Reed already?"

"Yeah, that's why I stopped by. Wanted to run some things past you." She sat in the armed chair in front of the contemporary steel-framed desk.

"So how'd it go? What'd he say?" She leaned against the edge of the desk, extended her model-length legs, crossed them at the ankles. "You learn anything new?"

"Actually I did. Did you know that men think of us as walking vaginas?"

"Get out!" She slapped Debra on the forearm.

"Are you being sarcastic?"

"No, I mean I know men think about sex a lot, but I had no idea they thought of us like that. Makes sense. What else did you learn?"

"Why the interest all of a sudden? You've been quite the pessimist throughout this process."

"I'm just curious. If he worked for Sherry and then works for you, maybe he knows what he's doing."

"You considering using his services?"

"Nope. I'm good." Rachel walked around the desk, sat in a burgundy, high-back leather chair, pressed the Call button. "Sylvia, please hold all calls."

"Oh, I get your undivided attention. I feel soooo special."

"Anyway," she swiveled in her chair, "what did you want to run past me?"

"Doc Reed said that I need to develop a list of needs and wants. You know, in a man."

"What do you want in a man?" Rachel tapped her Cross pen on the desk. "That's a great question."

"It really is. I would have never thought to write down character traits and qualities. I just kind of know what does and doesn't appeal to me."

"Here's where Sherry would say, 'Write the vision and make it plain,' and then break off into how everything is wonderful in her love life." Rachel leaned back in the chair, crossed, then uncrossed her arms. "I wonder if there's any validity to that. I use the concept for my agency with business plans, proposals and such."

"I'm going to try it. I have a mental checklist of things I learn after every failed relationship. Might as well put it on paper." She turned to an empty page in her notebook, drew a line down the middle. At the top of the left column, she wrote 'Must-Haves' and on the right, 'Preferences.'

"A checklist? A checklist of what?"

"From Johnny, I learned how to quickly defrost my front windshield. From Ronald, I learned how to bend chicken wings so the flapper stays flat and cooks evenly. And from Ke—"

"Okay, I get it. I'm not sure that's what the coach is

asking you for, but if it helps you recover from a sour ending, then do you." Rachel shook her head. "So how would you describe your perfect man?"

"He has to service me on a regular."

"Is that all you think about?"

"Uh, that's an affirmative."

"Well, put that on the 'Must-Have' side so we can move on to the stuff that really matters."

"Sex doesn't matter to you?"

"Of course it does, but what happens when you're not willing or worse yet able to make the beast with two backs? What's the foundation to sustain the relationship? If I relied solely on how Brian worked in the bedroom, I would've been gone a long time ago."

"So what's keeping you around?"

"Not what, who." She flicked her hair, placed a lock behind her right ear. "Conrad."

"Excuse me?"

"Conrad."

"You mean the not-so-cute guy who works for you?"

"Uh huh."

Debra shrugged, crinkled her forehead.

"He's my office husband."

Debra gasped, threw her hand over her mouth, spoke through her fingers. "Are you having an affair?"

"No, silly. He's my sounding board; my confidante."

Debra titled her head. "Humph, sounds like you're up to no good."

"It is totally innocent. Nothing like that. He is not my type, you know that."

"So why the whole office-husband thing?"

"I can talk to him without any pressure or concern for ulterior motive."

"And you can't talk to Brian?"

"Come on, now. You already know how strained our relationship is. Every conversation with Brian ends up as an argument about money, the kids or sex. Conrad helps me process through my business and personal matters in a neutral environment."

"How neutral? Crowne Plaza or Doubletree Inn?"

Rachel shook her head. "Did you not hear me say that it's not that kind of party? He's a good friend who lets me vent, gives sound advice and has my back. Dependable and trustworthy. An office husband."

"I'm still waiting for the venue of neutrality."

"My office, girl. We confer in my office with the door wide open. Geez!" She leaned toward Debra. "Unlike some people," she sat back in her chair, swiveled, "I'm not granting an all-access pass to my land of milk and honey."

Debra rolled her eyes. "You didn't even have to go there."

"You took me there."

"I'm just making sure you're levelheaded enough to help me assess the character of a good man."

"I can't make that call for you."

"And why not?"

"Because I won't be the one dating him. Besides, I'm not the best at picking men anyway."

"You are tripping. Brian is a great guy."

"Never said that he wasn't. I'm just not sure if he's the right guy for me. Eleven years into it and we still argue over the fact that I didn't change my last name." Her voice escalated as her hands became more animated. "I had a following of clients, suppliers and tons of pre-printed letterhead before we tied the noose, I mean knot. I wasn't about to waste mon—"

With her palms facing down, Debra lowered her hands

toward the floor. "Inside voice. I need you to use your inside voice."

"Oh, sorry. That still gets me going. Anyway, I don't need Doc Reed because I have my Conrad."

"*My* Conrad?"

"Oh, good grief. Conrad."

"Now for my list; I need your help."

"Oh, all right." Rachel huffed, turned on the projector, activated the screen to descend from a concealed ceiling panel.

"We don't need all that."

"You want my help or not? I need to see what we're working with."

"Well, I'm going to use the old-fashioned pen and paper."

"Do you." Rachel opened her laptop. "Okay, we have sex on a regular. What exactly is regular to you? Daily? Hourly?"

"Funny. How about three to four times a week."

"Carnal." She typed in the mandatory column. "How about the quality of sex?"

"Oh that's good. I want him to be creative, flexible, adventurous."

"Hold on, freak. I'm typing, not Sylvia. What about no falling asleep on top of you after sex?"

"I plan to put him to sleep every time. Put pillow talk as a preference." She scribbled her first entry in that column. "Employed is a must."

"Okay, if Doc Reed wants details does that mean he can be a pizza-delivery man?" She smirked. "Seriously, are you talking lower, middle or upper class? Blue-collar, white-collar?"

"Not doing the delivery-man thing again. I'm not so much concerned about whether he's labor or management, but he must earn at least seventy-thousand dollars; however, more is preferred. I'm not trying to deal with the my-woman-makes-more-money-than-me syndrome."

"Gotcha. So with that type of income, you're hoping that he has—"

"Health and life insurance, a reliable car, house or condo."

"Which leads to good credit."

"Yeah, yeah. No hidden fees like back taxes, bankruptcy, unpaid student loans or judgments. Pays his bills on time."

"What about his personality?"

Debra rubbed her chin. "Outgoing, friendly, charismatic with a great sense of humor. Secure and confident with a walk like Denzel." She leaned back in the chair, fanned herself with the paper.

"Okay, now you're on a roll. What about kids?"

"Lord, I'd say none as a must-have, but if he's my age, he probably has them."

"Grandkids, why you playin'? So you want him to be at least thirty-five years old?"

"Yep and no older than forty-five. I am not trying to change a grown man's diapers any time soon."

"I feel you on that one. So add childless as preferred."

"Now if he has kids, I have some conditions: no back child support, no baby-momma drama. He has to be a great father."

"What other family attributes?"

"He has to want at least two more children. Family oriented. Loves his mother, but not a momma's boy."

"It'd be great if his folks are happily married so that he has a model for a healthy relationship."

"Preference."

"Good." Rachel paused, tapped her index finger on her

mouth. "Ooooo, what about helping around the house? Not just yard work and broken appliances, but dishes, cleaning, laundry."

"An absolute must."

"Now I love a man who smells good and dresses like he stepped out of *Gentlemen's Quarterly*. So our ideal man has to be well-dressed. Not a hip-hop wanna be."

"*Our* man?" Debra sneered at Rachel. "Belted pants are critical. I do not want to know what brand of underwear he prefers."

"Boxers or briefs?"

"Boxer briefs. That's so stupid."

"How do you feel about a man who gets manicures and pedicures?"

"I'm okay with that. Actually, we can do dates at the spa on occasion. I will say that I am not looking to be in a relationship with a man who thinks that he is cuter than me. Too much vanity and fighting for mirror time."

"Dates. Put that on the must-have side. Brian and I don't date anymore. With the kids and both our careers, there's just not enough time."

"Yeah, dates and vacations. We have to take a real vacation at least once a year."

"I like that one."

Debra snapped her fingers. "I do not want a clingy man."

"You mean like Drew?"

"Lord, yes." She put her finger in the air. "But I don't want him traveling the globe and always away from home. I'm not trying to be a married single mom."

"Quality time, but not all the time. Got it."

"I'm not really a gift person, but I want to be surprised on occasion."

"With what? Jewelry? Candy? Clothes?"

"Yeah, all that and more. He has to remember the important dates, even if it's just a phone call or card."

Rachel looked off into the distance, sighed. "Romantic."

Together, they said, "Must-have," and then laughed.

"I'm a words-of-affirmation kind of gal so I need him to shower me with kind and encouraging words. Tell me that I'm beautiful even when I have sleep-crusted eyes and horrendous morning breath."

"L-I-A-R; got it." She looked at Debra, grinned. "Just kidding. We have a great list here." She zig-zagged the light from the electronic pointer across the screen. "I cannot believe that we haven't talked about his spirituality."

"OMG, as Aisha would say. Put this at the top of the must-haves. He has to be a God-fearing man with an intimate relationship with the Lord."

"Shame on us for missing that. You and your horny tail got us started on sex." Rachel rolled her eyes at Debra, flashed an insincere smile. "You want him to hold an office in the church?"

"He can be a minister or deacon, but definitely not an elder or pastor. I'm not trying to have late-night calls and needy folks zapping his virtue. He's got to be strong, focused, with stamina for s—"

"Back to carnality."

"That and I don't want to share him with everybody. Plus I am not trying to fight the front-pew hoochies who sit wide-legged with those short skirts."

Rachel revved up like she was about to deliver a sermon. "Now can I get an amen?"

"Amen and amen again!"

She nodded at Debra. "Thank ya, sistah!" Rachel coughed.

"That's what you get for mocking God's anointed."

She pressed the Call button. In a strained voice, she said, "Sylvia, water please," and then coughed again.

"You okay?" Debra stood.

Rachel put up her hand, nodded. After a couple more coughs, she said, "I'm good."

Sylvia entered with a chilled bottle of Evian. "Here you go, Ms. Nance. Will there be anything else?"

"No thank you." She took several swallows.

Sylvia turned to Debra. "Do you have need of anything?"

Debra shook her head, sat.

Sylvia exited the office.

Debra said, "She is so attentive. Add that to my list of requirements. Attentive; affectionate in public. I like holding hands and gentle kisses in public places."

"No busting slob?"

"You are so cross."

"I'm following your lead."

"A man who opens the door for me; gives me his jacket when I'm cold. A gentleman."

"Gentleman. Check." Rachel rapped her fingers on the laptop. "Now this next one is not from my own experience, but I have a girlfriend whose husband had psychological trauma from his childhood. Can't recall if it was hereditary or situational, but it destroyed their marriage."

"No childhood baggage; no meds." She looked at the lengthy list on the screen. "No wonder I'm single. I have so many requirements."

"You want what you want. Nothing wrong with having expectations. The problem comes in when you don't bring similar qualities. Marriage is not about bringing two half-people together to make a whole unit. If you aren't whole when you come in, you have a mess on your hands. You know I love numbers so what happens when you take fifty percent times fifty percent?"

Debra bit her lip, looked up to calculate the answer in her head.

"You get twenty-five percent. Now take one-hundred percent times itself and what do you get?" She looked at Debra, shook her head. "You get one-hundred percent. You're awful."

"Math is not my thing."

"Obviously."

"Why multiply anyway? I would've added."

"Because when you marry, you attach to the parents, siblings, in-laws," she said, as she smacked the back of one hand into the palm of the other. "All the ex-girlfriends, buddies and tons of life experiences that can be triggered by an innocent comment." Rachel shook her hands to alleviate the stingy sensation. "Heck, forget multiplying; it's an exponential situation. Remember what Sherry said about two becoming one flesh?"

"Yeah, but I didn't get it."

"Well, look at that Scripture from a mathematical perspective. One times one is one."

"One man, one woman, one flesh. Gotcha."

"Got another fleshy matter. It took me months to get Brian to leave the toilet seat down. Your butt ever hit that cold water at three in the morning? Not a good thing."

Debra shivered. "Add that please."

"Also add no snoring or snot rockets. No criminal record and by all means, he cannot be married."

"You are a nut. You know that, right?"

"Oh, I am soooo serious. What about his physical attributes?"

"Browner than me, but not dark chocolate."

"Give me Mandingo brown all day long. Mmm."

"Bring it back to me. You already have a man and he is not, I repeat, is not Mandingo brown."

"Whatever."

"I know I'm a little short, but—"

"A little. Didn't you say they called you Munchkin in high school?"

"I'm gonna need you to not conjure up those awful memories and stay focused on the task at hand."

"Just saying." She smirked.

"As I was saying, I want him to be at least five-eleven."

"Why not go for six feet? You've put everything else on the list."

"Not trying to be greedy. Conservative hair, no Mohawks, psychedelic colors or unkempt locks. Light facial hair. Maybe a mustache, but it has to be trimmed. No razor bumps and," she closed her eyes, paused, inhaled, exhaled, "bare chest."

"Tattoos?"

"Nothing on the face or neck and no weird body piercings, except for maybe his pe—"

"Gutter, gutter, gutter."

Chapter 12

Entreponegro

Days later, Debra returned to the North River Coffee House and took her place at her customary seat. She smiled when Angela brought chai tea and iced water to the table.

"I didn't think you saw me come in."

"Always," the restaurant manager said, as she walked back to the counter.

"Thanks."

She spoke over her shoulder, "You are more than welcome."

Debra pulled out her Dell laptop. She had tons of paperwork and online research to complete. Consumed with her work, she didn't hear the door chime that indicated a customer had entered the establishment. She swirled the tea to get every speck of the sweet spices, took the last swallow.

"Debra? Debra Hampton, is that you?"

She turned to see a handsome, yet unfamiliar, man standing near the dessert display. "Uh, hey, how are you?"

"You don't remember me, do you?" He walked toward her in a slow, orchestrated gait.

"No, I don't. Sorry." She flipped through the Rolodex in

her mind, came up empty. "Can you give me a hint?"

He smiled a gorgeous smile, said nothing.

"I seldom forget a face, but you don't look familiar to me. Did you go to Trotwood High School?"

"Nope."

"Madison Park Elementary? Roth Day Camp?"

"Nope and nope."

"Hmm, what's your name?"

"Jarrus Davis." He stood next to her.

Debra crinkled her forehead, rubbed it. "I can't recall ever meeting a Jarrus." She softened her countenance, gave a slight smile. "How do you know me?"

He pointed to her notebook. "Your name and number are written in big, bold letters."

She giggled. "That's so wrong." *Cute, but wrong.* His boyish face screamed 'I'm just out of college' but she took in his masculinity anyway. His soiled work clothes and dirty hands didn't overpower the subtleness of groomed fingernails, facial hair and Issey Miyake. "Yeah, my life is tied up in that book and since I'm a bit forgetful," she paused, shook her head, "I wanted it to be found if I should ever misplace it."

"So what's in there? How to keep the men at bay?"

If only you knew. "Mostly my undecipherable business notes."

"I knew there was something special about you."

"Because I scribble in a notebook?"

"No, because you're an attractive business woman." He touched his chin. "I don't often run into both brains and beauty. What are you drinking?"

"Chai tea."

He turned to Angela. "I'd like another chai tea for the lady."

Debra blushed, smiled. "Thank you."

"Your smile is beautiful."

She bowed her head.

"Aw come on now. My compliment is not something new to you. I'm sure you hear sweet things all of the time."

She smiled.

"So what is your business?"

Debra perked up, smiled wide. "Well, my business is event planning, but the job that pays bills is as a lawyer."

"Bet that keeps you busy."

"Pretty much."

"So when do you find time to relax?"

"Who has time to relax? I'm on a mission to make millions."

"As an attorney?"

"Nah, as an entreponegro."

"A what?"

"A Black entrepreneur," she said with a hint of you-should-know-that-one-dude attitude.

"I like that."

"Yeah, got that from a music artist. L-Marr, you ever heard of him?"

"Yeah, I have. Saw him do a set at the A-List Lounge and he rocked it."

"I know it. You should check him out at L-Marr.com. He just wrote and produced *City of Flight*. It's a tribute to Dayton, his birthplace. He's in a Hyundai commercial and now he's doing big things in Hotlanta."

"Really?" Jarrus steepled his fingers, touched his index fingers to his lips.

"Whatcha thinking about?"

"Just wondering how long you're going to make me stand here, before you invite me to sit with you."

"Oh, I'm sorry. Please take a seat."

Jarrus moved the chair that was opposite Debra to sit next to her.

Debra smiled. "You study nonverbal communication? Moving the chair to the adjacent versus opposing position is a let-me-reduce-barriers-to-communication move."

"That and I want to sit closer to you. You smell wonderful."

She blushed. "Before this goes any further, you need to know that I'm a bit older than I look."

"What are you? Twenty-four, twenty-five?"

"Ha! Not quite. How old are you?"

"Twenty-eight."

She sucked in air through her teeth. "Ooo, you're a young 'un."

"Age doesn't matter to me. I know what I like."

Flattered, she touched her chest, batted her lashes, smiled.

"I bet I can guess your weight within three pounds."

She spanned her arms to offer a full view of her petite frame, turned to the left, then right. "Guess."

"Give me a hug."

"A hug? You're direct." She relaxed her arms.

"No, so I can gauge your weight. Honest, nothing more."

She stood.

Jarrus put his muscular arms around her waist, from a seated position he lifted her. "A buck ten." He placed her squarely on the ground.

"I am impressed. One twelve." She started to pull out the chair.

"Let me get that for you."

"Thank you." She sat, propped her elbows on the table, rested her chin on interlaced fingers.

"All right, I win the bet."

"I don't recall discussing a wager."

"How about dinner?"

Walking vagina. Walking vagina. Walking vagina. "I'm not too sure about that."

"Who broke your heart?"

She snapped, "Why do I have to have a broken heart?"

"I can see it in your eyes."

She turned away, tensed.

He leaned toward her to look into her eyes, cupped his hands around hers. "I can help you through that pain."

Debra wanted to pull away, but something about his voice, his touch, soothed her. She squirmed in the chair.

"Didn't mean to make you uncomfortable." He leaned back.

"No, you're good." She relaxed.

"Hate to leave you like this, but I have to get back to working for the man." He reached for his wallet, handed Debra his business card. "I'm a great listener. Call me."

She rummaged through her purse for her card holder and then handed Jarrus her business card. "You call me."

He stood, caressed her back, said, "I enjoyed talking with you. Let's stay in touch."

She giggled. "I'd like that." She watched Jarrus walk away and wondered if she'd ever see him again.

Chapter 13

Killjoy

Excited about the interaction with Jarrus, Debra called Rachel. When she learned that her friend was out of the office with a client, Debra called Doc Reed.

"Hey, Doc. This is Debra."

"Hey, Debra. How are you?"

A full smile washed across her face. "I'm good."

"I can hear you smiling through the phone. What's going on?"

"I just met the most wonderful guy."

"That's interesting. How's your list coming along?"

"He's wonderful. Witty, intelligent, great conversationalist." She took a moment to relive the chat.

"Intriguing. Your list?"

"Can you allow me a few minutes to bask in the glory of our exchange?"

"If you're looking for someone to be giddy over this guy, you've called the wrong person."

"You were my second choice."

"I'm flattered." He inhaled a deep breath, exhaled. "He said and did all the right things. Without missing a beat, he tapped into each of the five love languages: words of affirmation, acts of service, quality time, gifts and physical touch."

"Well, uh—"

"He spent a few minutes talking with you; complimented your appearance; touched you in a non-sexual way; offered to help you with something—hold the door maybe—"

"He pulled out the chair for me."

"Uh huh and he gave you something. Nothing significant; possibly a piece of gum...."

"A cup of coffee."

"Bingo!"

"Okay, so you've proven your point. You know men. That doesn't mean that you know this man. He said that he enjoyed our conversation."

"Did you give him your number?"

"We exchanged numbers."

"Then he should be calling soon."

"How long do I wait to call him?"

"You mean after he calls you?"

"No, I mean if he doesn't call. What's the appropriate lapse of time so that I don't appear needy, but still keep his interest?"

"Never."

"Maybe I didn't explain myself correctly. We had the best dialogue I've had in months."

"I understand and I'm not trying to steal your joy. I want to show you how the emotional component can skew your judgment. Trust me. If he doesn't call, then he wasn't as interested as he led you to believe."

"But his words and actions indicated that he—"

"Don't listen to anything he says. He wants your goody box and will say or do anything to get it. He's wired that way. Keep your guard up. His maturity level may not be such that he can keep his animal at bay."

"I feel like I'm playing a game."

"Either play the game or be the game."

"You mean be in the game."

"No, be the game. Men are natural-born hunters who see the thrill of pursuing the goody box like taking down the prize buck. They adapt to its environment, mimic mating calls, even go as far as to use deer urine to attract it. Why? To get close enough to shoot it; tap it; hit it; whatever you want to call it."

"Then quit it."

"Exactly. The prize is displayed over the mantle as another win to brag about to his friends."

Debra sighed. "That is so awful. Women are not animals and men shouldn't treat us like that."

"A man's identity is tied to his goody-box conquests. That's why locker-room talk is a measure of his stature. Brag on your Johnson as a competitive force."

"Who would've ever thought?"

"Our focus is to keep you from repeating the pattern. The longer you hold off the goody box, the more emotionally invested he becomes."

"The elusive deer that gets out of his crosshairs."

"Now you're feeling it. He's on a mission to capture the goody box and then go on to the next game. But if his heart gets involved, he can't just walk away. Hold on a second."

Debra mumbled, reached for her notebook, jotted a few things.

"Okay, I'm back. We have to wrap this up. I'm going out on a date."

"Aww, how romantic. I'm sure your wife loves that."

"I'm going on a date with my daughters."

"You take your daughters on dates?"

"Yeah, we'll talk more about that next time. Back to hunting. You gotta make him work for it. Right now, you are a wounded doe. You need time to recover from past hurts, build up your strength and endurance so that you can RUN!" He laughed.

"That's not funny."

"Seriously though, as long as you are wounded, you are easy prey."

Debra huffed.

"Not easy as in sleazy easy, but easy as in unguarded, defenseless."

"But what if Jarrus doesn't attempt to track me?"

"I like the hunting symbolism, but—"

"I'm going to spend extra time at the coffee house and hopefully run into him again."

"Not good. That's all emotional stuff. He tickled your eyes and ears and now you are trying to position yourself for another chance encounter."

"Never thought of it like that."

"Well, that's what it is. This request will be difficult for you, but I know that you have enough stamina to do it."

"Oh, Lord." She readied her pen to capture the relationship nugget.

"If he does call and asks you out on a date, don't accept the offer."

"Say what? I'm sitting here waiting on him to call me and you want me to play hard to get?"

"I'm telling you I know how he's wired. It's all about the chase. You want this thing to be different, right?"

"Yes." She let the word linger until she sounded like a hissing snake.

"Take the desire from his eyes and groin to his heart.

Women process eyes, heart, groin. The only way it's going to work long-term is to meet at the heart. That means you'll have to wait until his heart catches up with yours. Your heart kicks in at Phase Two, while his at Phase Three."

"Matching hearts, mix-matched phases. What the devil?"

To minimize Debra's confusion, he said, "Let's try this analogy: Your destination is California. You've planned the trip for you and your man, packed your bags. You're in a hurry to get there, so you booked a non-stop flight."

"Hmmm."

"You arrive in a few hours, you're checking your watch, pacing the floor, wondering why he hasn't gotten there yet all the while he's still in Dayton at the bus terminal waiting for a Greyhound to make the week-long cross-country journey."

"Good illustration, Doc. The ultimate destination is the same, but how and when we arrive differs." She nodded. "Wait on him to catch up, huh? It sounds reasonable, but I'm afraid to put it to the test. What if it doesn't work?"

"You're no worse off. But what if it does? Look, you can do what you want, I'm only here to advise. The decision is yours, but if you keep doing what you've always done...."

"Yeah, yeah, yeah. But if I play hard to get, he will lose interest."

"He may. Some men aren't willing to put in the time, energy and effort to chase the goody box because it comes to them so easily."

Debra twirled her index finger like a maestro conducting an orchestra. "So you're saying that women have created these monstrous men who follow the wham-bam-thank-you-ma'am mantra?"

"No, but I am saying that women have enabled men by making the goody box readily available. If he's not willing to

110

invest in you, he's not worth it."

"But then I run the risk of being alone."

"But," he paused for emphasis, "you'll have your dignity."

"Yeah, me and dignity home alone again."

Chapter 14

Girls' Night Out

Sherry walked into the office to find Roxanne hovering at her desk. She thought about turning around and pretending like she didn't see her, but decided to confront the levitating leviathan.

Roxanne watched Sherry approach the desk. At an inappropriately loud volume, she said, "Why haven't you answered my pages?"

"Because I knew what you wanted." She placed the clipboard full of worksheets and numbers on the desk.

Roxanne looked at her, waited for her to read her mind.

"You want me to tag that material on the dock so the truck can deliver it to the warehouse."

Roxanne nodded. "So why didn't you tag it?"

"You tell me why?" Sherry took off her safety glasses, looked Roxanne in the eyes.

"Excuse me?"

"You heard me, why do you think I haven't tagged the inventory?"

Roxanne stuttered.

"Let me help you. I finally got a decent handle on this job, without much guidance from you, and now you have me covering for Sara while she's on vacation."

"So?"

"So, I'm going to make sure that both jobs are right. My focus is on ordering parts to keep the plant running versus housekeeping. If you don't like my prioritization, then tell me how else to do it."

"I suppose you took the best approach."

"Thank you very much. I'll tag the dock after I go to the restroom and call the suppliers. If that's not sufficient, feel free to tag it yourself."

Roxanne bowed her head, tucked her tail and proceeded to the dock.

After relieving herself, Sherry checked her voice messages. She had eight calls from suppliers, two from the warehouse and one from Debra.

Using a deep-South drawl, Debra's message said, "Sherry, we goin' escape the plantation t'night. Follow the drinking gourd. We'z goin' north t'night. Escape that mean slave master, girl. Escape! Escape!" She reverted to her normal voice. "Hey, lady, call me when the slave master isn't watching you."

With tears streaming down her face, Sherry called Debra.

"Good afternoon, Debra Hampton speaking."

Sherry erupted into laughter. "Girl, if you aren't the stupidest thing. That was hilarious." She paused to catch her breath. "Thanks for making me laugh. Medusa has lost her ever-loving mind."

"And you are just the one to help her find it."

"She's pushing me to go ghetto on her and I so don't want to do that, but if I have to…."

"You will."

"Right. And it's not like they're going to fire me. My last

day is April first."

"Wow. I'm sorry that you're losing your job."

"Thanks, but it's not lost. I know exactly where it's going. Mexico!"

They laughed.

Debra said, "I called earlier to see if you wanted to go out Friday. I need to unwind and I miss my girls."

"I'm there. Just tell me when and where."

~ ~ ~ ~ ~ ~ ~

Rachel and Debra arrived together at the Therapy Café— an eclectic downtown establishment that caters to the mature crowd.

The friends had come straight from work. After a makeup touch up, change of jewelry and shoes and unbuttoning a couple buttons, their business attire transformed to let's-get-this-party-started clothes. They sat in the first set of seats facing the stage.

Debra felt her hair to make sure the spikes were still erect. "Who's performing tonight?"

"I don't know, but I'm sure they're good."

"So what's the 411 on you and Brian?"

"Geez. Can't I get a couple of drinks in me before you beat me over the head?"

Debra waved over the waitress. "Place your order."

"Strawberry daiquiri, please. Hold the whip cream."

"Water with lemon for now. Thank you." She turned to Rachel. "Okay, spit it out."

"Your persistence is a nuisance."

Debra smiled, laid her left arm across her stomach, propped her right elbow on the prostrate arm, rested her chin on her hand. "I'm listening."

"I don't know where to start. It sounds cliché, but Brian and I have grown apart." She waited for Debra's facial expression to change. When it didn't, she continued. "Somewhere in this journey, I emotionally disconnected from him."

"Somewhere? You really don't know?"

"I can't put it on any one incident. Like most marriages, we've had a lot of trying times."

Debra affirmed with a nod.

"His family is as dysfunctional as mine, but at least my people love each other. His parents are cool, but the rest of the crew...." She rested her head on the back of the chair. "The bad part about it is that I need that connection."

"That's what your girls are here for."

She lifted her head. "I love you much, but I need the attention of a man."

"You have the attention of a man; a great man."

"I know. The little infractions were awful in and of themselves, but I totally checked out when that whole thing went down with his brother."

A year prior, Michael—Brian's older brother—came to live with the Monroes. In the midst of a tumultuous divorce, Michael needed a place to lay his head and store the few belongings his estranged wife hadn't destroyed. Having two grown men and an assertive woman living in the same house proved to be a challenging adjustment. Michael's dictatorship commands didn't set well with Rachel. He often barked orders at her, yelped at the kids and howled if he had to wait too long for dinner.

On several occasions, Rachel asked Brian to talk to his brother. She didn't want to incite a riot between siblings, but she was not going to be disrespected in her home, especially when she was paying the three-thousand dollar mortgage.

Brian said, "Aw, Rach. His bark is worse than his bite. He's always been a loud talker. He doesn't mean anything by it. Besides, he's really hurting. It's just for a couple more weeks."

"I understand that he's hurting, but that doesn't justify his actions. My mother wouldn't come in here and talk to me like he does, so what makes him think it's okay for him to do it?"

"Rach."

"Rach, nothing. If you don't handle his foolishness, then I will."

A couple more weeks seasoned into two months. One night with the family sitting at the dinner table, the discussion migrated to the bullies who had threatened Marcus.

BJ said, "Mommy, I stopped those bullies from pushing Marcus."

"Very good, baby. I'm glad you're a great big brother."

He smiled an accomplished smile.

"I went to the school. The principal has a meeting scheduled with your father and me as well as those boys' parents." She rubbed Marcus' back. "They only pick with you because you're smaller than they are, baby."

Brian said, "And it's two of them. Twin brothers, right?"

Rachel nodded. "They're a year older than Marcus and the biggest things in the school. They're almost as tall as the teacher. No wonder he's intimidated."

Michael snapped at Marcus. "Quit being a punk and whip them boys!" Taller and much more muscular than Brian, Michael loomed over Marcus by almost three feet. Between the growl and size differential, he may as well have been a grizzly bear pouncing on a frightened rabbit. Yet another bully.

Marcus jumped from the table and ran upstairs. BJ and Charisse cried. Rachel looked at Brian. Nothing.

"Come on kids. Let's get ready for bed." She took the children upstairs, calmed them down and prepped them for bed. Thirty minutes later she returned to the kitchen. Brian and Michael were still at the table.

"I am fed up to here," she stretched her arm north, "with your outbursts and demands, Michael. I know that things are tough for you, but you will not raise your voice to me or my children again."

He glared up at her, waved her off, expelled a puff of air.

"I know you didn't just blow me off." She looked at Brian for reinforcement.

"Babe, calm down, relax. Let's talk about this."

"Don't tell me to calm down and time for talking is over." She turned to Michael. "It's time for you to leave. You have until tomorrow evening to pack your things and get out of my house."

"This is my brother's house and I will leave when he tells me to leave."

"I don't think you fully understand. This is my queendom," she pointed to the floor, "and you have worn out your welcome."

Michael crossed his arms, rocked in the chair.

"If I have to tell you again, I'll call the police to escort you out."

Michael stood. He pushed the chair back and it crashed to the floor.

Rachel jumped back.

With rage in his eyes, Michael swelled his chest, walked up on her.

Mogli stood guard in front of Rachel and snarled at Michael.

She looked around the mastodon that trumpeted over her at Brian who was in the process of standing. Her children's faces flashed in her mind. Like a lioness protecting her cubs, she stared down Michael. Her chest heaved.

In what seemed to be slow motion, Michael punched the wall inches from her face. He stood over her for a moment and then stormed out of the house.

Rachel fell to the floor.

Brian ran to her side. "Rach, are you okay?" He rubbed her face.

"Why didn't you help me?"

"It happened so fast. I didn't expect him to…." He shook his head to clear the memory.

"You didn't even make an effort." Tears splattered on her lap.

"He's never lashed out like that before." He wiped her eyes, helped her stand.

Her knees buckled. "Oh, I need to sit down."

Brian assisted her to the chair and then walked to the sink to get her a glass of water. "Why did you threaten to call the police?" He set the water on the table.

Between sobs, she said, "Because you weren't going to do anything to protect me or your children."

"But you know that's what his wife did. You set him off."

"I cannot believe that you're blaming this on me. He came at me with his fist balled and you did absolutely nothing."

At that moment, the smidgen of respect Rachel had for her husband evaporated. She emotionally shut down, closed her heart and constructed an impenetrable force field to repel attempts to infiltrate.

The adult crowd trickled into the Therapy Café for a night of smooth jazz. The waitress set the drinks on the coffee table.

"Thanks." Debra squeezed lemon juice in her water,

stirred it with the straw. "Yeah, that was awful."

"And I don't know how to move past it. I didn't need him to take care of me and until he talked me into having kids, I didn't even need his seed. But the one thing I needed, he let me down, over and over."

"Having your back?"

"Right. You wouldn't think it'd be such a big deal, but with all the men in my life letting me down, he exacerbated an already awful situation."

"So you're holding him accountable for the actions of other men?"

"No, I'm holding him accountable for his actions. If things had played out differently, I wouldn't be having this conversation with you. I know he's a great guy, but hurt on top of hurt isn't good."

"Makes you vulnerable."

"Vulnerable and gullible, a dangerous combination."

"You gullible? Get out of here."

"Let me tell you something, I may be great in the boardroom, but when it comes to relationships and playing that game, I'm a loser every time."

"How can you say that? Brian is a great catch."

"Sure he was, eleven years ago. I don't know if I've contaminated him or if he's always been this man, but I'm just not feeling him anymore. Can I be honest with you?"

"Of course."

"If it weren't for the kids, I probably would have been gone by now."

"Wow, Rachel. I had no idea."

"I'm torn, Debra. Here I am a decision-maker closing multi-million-dollar deals and I can't decide whether to stay or go."

"Stay, honey. Ain't nothing out here."

"If you say so. I've probably lived almost half my life. I don't want to live the last half miserable. I'd rather be single and alone than married and lonely."

"So what are you doing to cope?"

"Hanging with my girls." She smiled.

"That's obviously not enough."

Rachel bowed her head. "It's gotten so bad that I went online to track down some of my college buddies." She lifted her head. "Found a couple of them on Facebook and paid a couple dollars to find two others."

"What in the world?"

"I needed to connect with someone who knew the old Rachel. I have changed so much over the past few years I wanted to know if they'd recognize me."

"Did they?"

"Most of them. A couple of my," she gestured quote-unquote, "partners noticed a change."

"Really? Just by talking on the phone?"

"Yep, one even asked me where his friend was because I couldn't be her."

"Get out."

"I'm serious."

"So did he say what was different about you?"

"I'd rather not say."

"Come on."

"Nope."

"That's so wrong."

"Oh well, wrong I will be."

"What about your other partner? What did he say?"

"He was so encouraging. He helped me focus on today and laugh at yesterday." She smiled, rubbed her hands together. "He introduced me to jazz. We used to listen to Miles Davis, Wynton Marsalis and Herbie Hancock, eat popcorn and caress each other's hands for hours at a time."

"That sounds so romantic."

"It was. I miss him. It's a good thing he's in Michigan or...."

"Or what?"

"Just know that I'm aware of my vulnerability and I'm keeping my past loves at bay."

"Two-hundred-mile minimum."

"At the absolute minimum." She shook her head. "I am bored with marriage."

"How can you be bored? You're always on the go with the kids and work."

"Busy work, girl. 'Cause if I'm not busy, I get depressed thinking about my life. I love my family, don't get me wrong, but it hasn't played out like I had envisioned."

"Isn't it something how on the outside we look like we have it together, but on the inside we're empty?"

"Dead man walking. Walking the green mile. Walking the green mile."

"Call me zombie."

They laughed.

"Enough about me. How's it going with Doc Reed?"

"He's telling me to hold out on sex, but I need it. You think his plan will work if I hold out on one and have another one to take care of this monkey on my back?" She crossed her legs, slipped off a stiletto and let it dangle on the tip of her toes. "If the best time to find a job is when you already have one, then the best time to find a man is when you already have one too, right?"

"Now you know that's a hoochie move?" She nodded toward Debra's feet.

"What? I'm just letting my feet get some air."

"Uh huh. It's getting hot in here." She nodded toward a

pack of wolves salivating at the bar. "They've been over there ogling you all night."

"How do you know it's me they're gawking over and not you?"

"Because every time you bounce that shoe, you expose a little more of your promised land."

"Girl, why didn't you tell me?"

"Thought that was what you were trying to do."

"I'm horny, not hoochie."

"Too late. Here comes one now."

"Hi." In one choreographed move, he spun the chair around, straddled the seat and rested his elbows on the chair back. "I'm Harold." He exposed a mouthful of gold teeth.

Rachel and Debra struggled to stifle the explosion of laughter that churned in their bellies.

Rachel flashed her three-carat diamond ring. "Hi, Harold. We're waiting on our husbands."

"My bad." He stood, spun around, hopped like Morris Day. "Holla." He gestured the peace sign and then walked away.

"Can you believe Sexual Chocolate? I must be giving off a scent that says 'I'm searching for a man' because I attract a lot more lately."

"Anyone worth mentioning?"

"Yeah, Jarrus."

"That's the guy from the coffee house, right?"

"Yeah."

"So how's it going?"

"It's not. He hasn't called me."

"So call him."

"No can do."

"And why not?"

"Because Doc Reed s—"

"Are you really going to follow his advice and take the chance on missing out on a great guy?"

"A wise friend once said to me that if it ain't broke, don't fix it."

"That would be me."

"Well, my friend, this thing is broke and needs major repair."

"That White guy in the band has been checking you out."

"I'm not sure that I can do that. I prefer chocolate."

"Don't knock it 'til you try it."

Debra looked at Rachel.

"What? I haven't been married all my life."

"You played that funky music with a White guy?"

Rachel sipped her daiquiri.

"What about his—"

"Don't believe the lie. That's all I have to say."

"Now who's the freak?" Debra's countenance mellowed. "What's wrong?"

"Just had a Vincent moment. I miss him."

"Do you miss him or do you miss his loving?"

"A little of both."

"Girl, bye. You miss that loving. You know good and well that Vincent was just trying to get the most buck for his bang."

"You mean the most bang for his buck?"

"I said what I meant to say. All he knows how to do is get paid for using his golden rod."

"He does have the Midas touch."

"Maybe so, but good loving doesn't make him a good man."

"This is true."

Sherry walked into the restaurant, paused at the door, looked for her friends. She spotted them in the lounge area and then walked to them.

"Hey, ladies." She hugged her girls. "Sorry I'm late."

Debra said, "Evilene?"

"You know it. She had a last minute job she just had to have done today."

Rachel said, "Sherry, you look wonderful. I'm loving that dress."

Sherry blushed. "Just a little something Dwight picked out for me."

"I had no idea you had such shapely legs."

"I didn't until I started all that dang-blasted walking at work." She pointed her toe like a ballerina, did her version of a pirouette.

Debra patted the seat next to her. "And the hair; you go, girl."

"Thought I'd give the curly locks a break and go for the straight look."

Rachel stood. "Welcome to year twenty-ten, sweetie."

"That's so mean." Sherry sat. "Don't get used to this. I'm back to little corporate Annie on Monday."

Debra said, "Why? You should go in all dolled up and really work Roxanne's nerves."

Rachel nodded. "You ladies want anything? I'm headed to the ladies' room and then the bar."

"I'll take two orders of crab cakes and a Long Island iced tea."

"Debra, do you want anything?"

"Yeah, can you order me some chicken quesadillas and a Cosmopolitan?"

"Will do."

Debra turned toward Sherry. "I really think that you should keep that look. It takes ten years off of you."

"Too much maintenance for this conservative chick. I

need to keep it simple."

"Dwight may be giving you a subtle hint to cross over."

Sherry paused, pondered. "You might be right. He was so sweet in his approach. He didn't insult or criticize, he just said, 'Babe, I love it when you wear your hair straight.'"

"When was your hair straight?"

"After I had gotten off work and had sweated out the curls."

"Now that's funny."

"I know." She pulled a compact from her purse, primped in the tiny mirror. "I do like it. I feel beautiful."

"You've always been beautiful. A new dress and hairstyle didn't create that."

"Aw, thanks. That's why I love you."

"Love you, too." Debra hugged her friend. "Now back to Count Blacula; what's the latest?"

"Let me tell you what Elvira did today." She moved the chair to sit closer to Debra. "Now you know my job is phasing out right?"

"Right, right."

"Well, my last day was supposed to be April first."

Debra gasped, threw her hand over her mouth. "She's letting you go sooner?"

"No. This dingbat complained to the president that she couldn't handle all the work by herself."

"Wasn't she the one who told HR that she no longer needed you?"

"Yep, makes sense to everyone but her. Anyway, the president asked her why was she letting me go, if she couldn't do the work. Apparently, he told her that he knew that I could get the job done and instructed her to keep me until June first."

"So you have two more months?"

"Yep. God is good."

"That's wonderful." She scratched her ankle. "Or is it? That means you have to deal with Dr. Funkystein a little longer."

"Yes and no. I'm not working for her anymore, but I'm keeping the same desk."

"Oh, that's good. She's really going to be mad now. I'm loving it."

"You really need to learn how to not be so vengeful."

Rachel returned to the table with three drinks. "The waitress will bring over the food when it's ready."

Debra caught Rachel up on Sherry's news.

Rachel said, "Why don't you just quit and find a job?"

"I've decided I'm going to shift my career all together."

"Doing what?"

"Going to finish my MBA and then use all these corporate skills to help small business owners."

"Where'd that desire come from?"

"I come from a long line of entrepreneurs. Mayo; Wheat; Bowman; they're all relatives. It's time to do me."

"But what about the money? How will you make it until your business is self-sufficient?"

Debra tapped Rachel on the arm. "Did you forget who you're talking to? Ms. Frugal has probably saved up a bazillion dollars."

"I wish. I do have some money put away and getting a little something from Oracle." She noticed a guy at the bar, smiled.

Rachel tapped on Sherry's forehead. "Hello? Sherry, are you in there?"

"Oh, sorry. Got distracted. What was I saying?"

"You were telling us about that fine brother over there who's been cheesing at you since he walked in."

Sherry looked everywhere but in the direction of the hottie at the bar. "Who? Where?"

Debra said, "Don't even try it."

Rachel said, "He is cute now. You should go talk to him." She nudged Sherry with her elbow.

"Nah, that's okay. Not my style."

"Oh, not Dwight you mean."

Sherry stood. "I have to go to the restroom. I'll be right back."

Debra and Rachel watched Sherry walk away.

"Is it my imagination or is she switching her booty?"

Debra chuckled. "Not your imagination. She is working the hallway like the runway." She called out, "Work it, Sherry."

Without looking back, Sherry waved off her girlfriend and then faded to black.

Debra said, "We should plan a trip to celebrate Sherry's transition."

"That's a great idea. I could use some excitement and a change of scenery."

"Wait just a minute, Stella. We aren't taking this trip for you to get your groove back."

"Would you stop it? I'm cool."

"That's what you say now Mrs. I-put-out-an-APB-to-fix-my-broken-heart."

"Cancel the noise. I know the perfect place."

"Where?"

"Montego Bay, Jamaica."

"Oh, boy. Do you do anything small scale?"

"Ha! Now you forgot who you're talking to."

Chapter 15

Daddy Dates

Debra looked over Downtown Dayton from her corner office. As part of her morning work ritual, she watched commuters and pedestrians scurry and then singled out one person. She followed their movement until no longer in view all the while wondering who they were, where they came from and where they were headed. The process relaxed her before the day got hectic.

Her thoughts were interrupted by the Bluetooth headset buzzing in her ear. She hurried to the desk, rummaged through her purse looking for the phone. The auto-answer feature accepted the call.

"Good morning, Debra Hampton."

"Well good morning, Ms. Hampton," Doc Reed said. "So I get the professional greeting today, huh?"

"Hey, Doc. I couldn't get to my cell to see who was calling, so I used my corporate voice just in case you were a client." She revved up like Martin Payne from the 1990s sitcom, *Martin*. "Whazzup?"

"Just calling to check on your progress."

"Oh, so you do phone calls in non-emergency situations too?"

"Sure do. This process is going to take some time and it's my job—my passion—to see it through to the end. Anything new with Jarrus?"

"Nope."

"Stand your ground."

"I know; don't call." She reclined back in her chair. "Last time we talked, you were on a date with your daughters. That is so cute."

"I guess from a woman's perspective, it is cute, but that's not my intention."

"Why do you do it?"

"In my coaching, I've seen lots of women who are carrying hurt from their childhood into relationships."

"From absent fathers and deadbeat dads?"

"That and from fathers who don't teach their girls about men."

"I thought that a father in the home was a good thing."

"It's a great thing, but just being there isn't enough. Most fathers focus on provision for the family and oftentimes overlook their role in nurturing and instruction."

"I'm listening."

"A father is a son's first hero and a daughter's first love. The hero part comes natural between a man and his son because men thrive on respect. But the love thing; it takes more effort."

"And that's why I don't expect anything from men. As my girlfriend said, 'You can't fault a dog for doing what dogs do.'"

"Hold on now. Are you saying that men are dogs?"

"If it looks like a dog and acts like a dog," she rolled her eyes, pursed her lips, "then it's a dog."

"That's not fair. Men are wired for respect. Nowhere in the Bible does it tell a man to respect his wife because it's natural for him."

"Hmm."

"And nowhere does God command women to love their husbands. It's just what you do. But in Ephesians, God tells women to revere their husbands. Cut out all the gooseneck, hands on hips, manipulation. It undermines a man's self-esteem. And He tells us to love our wives as Christ loved the church. Why? Because it goes outside of our nature."

"I never looked at it like that."

"So men are not dogs, at least not all of them, it's just that God designed us for respect as a primary motivator and love is secondary."

"Amazing."

"Women are love first, then—"

"Then respect."

"Very good, Luke Skywalker. You are learning."

"That's so stupid. You're Yoda now?"

"I am the master teacher of relationships."

"You are making me a believer." Debra leaned forward, grabbed a notepad and pencil. "So why don't fathers teach these things to their daughters? I mean my dad explained the mechanics of sex: ovaries, uterus, penis." She paused, smiled. "But not all this stuff."

"Most men don't want to think of their precious daughters as objects of lustful desire and they aren't comfortable having that type of conversation. Lots of men can't communicate the emotional component."

"Because they aren't wired that way."

"Exactly. And some just don't think it's important."

"Awful. So why don't mothers prepare their daughters?"

"I can only teach you as much as I know."

"Duh, that makes sense."

"It's my job to teach you what your father didn't tell you

and your mother didn't know."

"That's a shame."

"What? That I'm here to teach you?"

"No, that you *have* to teach me."

"Well, it keeps me gainfully employed, but I'd rather have folks healed than have to go through the stuff I hear about. So, back to my daughters, that's why I do what I do with them. I use the dates as a means to an end."

"It's not about quality time?"

"Of course it is and a whole lot more. I'm showing them how a man should treat them on a date. Let's take Samara for example. After conferring with her parents—my wife and I discuss the arrangements for the daddy-daughter dates—her would-be suitor will pick her up at home. Blowing his car horn from the driveway won't do. He opens the car door for her and then drives to a restaurant where his acts of chivalry continue. He opens doors, helps her to her seat, makes sure she's comfortable. Following light conversation and the meal, *he* pays and then drives her home. He escorts her to the front door and at most, he kisses her on the forehead or cheek. From there, they part ways. No overnight stays or late-night rendezvous."

Debra scribbled on the paper. "I guess the dates are training sessions."

"My commitment to fatherhood is to show my girls who they are and fill their emotional love tank."

"Kind of like Jarrus was feeling me out to find out what makes me tick?"

"Exactly. If Samara knows that she is motivated by words of affirmation and I have poured into her, then she won't be smitten by every joker who comes along with good game. As long as she knows that's her button, she won't respond out of emotion when he pushes it."

"The emotion thing again."

"That's how most women work. Now I have a couple of female clients who are more logical than emotional. They process information like a man and can control their feelings to a point, but they still have the emotional component."

"Sounds like Rachel. Her personal life is in total chaos, but she can still function at maximum capacity at work."

"She's compartmentalized or fragmented her situation. That's a man thing. But if she doesn't rein it in soon, she's going to have an eruption."

"Don't speak that on her."

"Calling it like I see it."

"How old are your girls?'

"Samara is seven and Sheree is five."

"So other than the dates, how do you teach them about relationships?"

"I use visuals."

"You mean diagrams of the human anatomy?"

"Uh, no. That's the mechanical stuff. I'm dealing with the emotional aspect of relationships and I use age-appropriate visuals."

"Like?"

"Okay, I used a pitcher of water, an empty glass and food coloring to explain how Daddy loves them. I rattled off a few things that I do to show them that I love them, each time adding a little more water to the glass. Then I asked them what things Daddy does to make them feel loved. When Samara said that our weekly dates make her happy, I added water. Sheree said that our evening prayers are important to her, so I added more water. By the time we finished talking about all the things I do that lets them know Daddy loves them, the water was spilling onto the table."

"Ah, gotcha. You filled them to the brim."

"Right and since the glass was full—symbolic of their love tank—there wasn't room for anyone to add to it."

"So where does the food coloring come in?"

"I wanted to emphasize how other things will be presented that will taint the purity of the water. I added several colors of food coloring, created a dark concoction and offered it to them to drink."

"Good stuff."

"Of course they didn't drink it. If I don't fill that void, then it may be a man, drugs or some other addictive behavior that they use as an attempt to compensate and comfort the emptiness."

"Oh, that's good." Debra clicked the mechanical pencil to drop more lead.

"I'm the first protector of my daughters' goody boxes, so I'm teaching them techniques that will help them avert the stressors of dating. I know that I can't shield them from everything, but it's my duty to prepare them for battle."

"You make it sound like dating is confrontational."

"Hmm, now let's think about that. How would you label your last few encounters?"

Debra threw her hands in the air, pushed away from the desk, expelled a sigh. "Whatever."

"I'm just saying; if you're not prepared, then you'll end up a wounded soldier."

"I'm an amputee hobbling without a crutch, why you playin'?"

"Battle scars, purple heart and worst of all, post-traumatic stress disorder."

"You are good."

"Nightmares, disoriented, flashbacks…."

"Okay, okay, I got it." She grabbed the desk, pulled herself back to the writing position. "I'm mad that I'm just learning this stuff. My dad was a great provider. He taught me about the mechanics of sex, but I can't recall us ever talking about the emotions."

"Yep, those soul ties are powerful. And don't forget the spiritual component."

"Now that I think about it, I wasn't a daddy's girl like some of my friends. My smile or cute little ways didn't get me any extra attention. It came from my mom."

"That's perceptive of you."

"So I'm vulnerable to men who compliment me and express adoration because that's my love language and my tank wasn't filled as a child?"

"Ding, ding, ding. We have a winner."

"That's so stupid."

"Stupid, but true. Your relationship with your father affects your dating practices. You are so focused on getting your ego stroked that you lose sight of the big picture."

"You sound like a philosopher."

"Nah, I'm not a philosopher; just a spiritual cardiologist. I love to get to the heart of the matter."

"Ha! That's good. How did you become so proficient in relationships?"

"It really is a God-given gift. The dynamics have always intrigued me, so I observed people to figure out why they do what they do. It's really simple, once you get it."

"Like taking the red pill in *The Matrix*."

"Exactly. Once the truth was revealed to Neo, he could defend himself against the agents."

"That was a great movie."

"Since you want to use movies to relate this principle, recall that Neo's training took time. He had a series of defeats and disappointments."

"Yeah, but once the code was revealed, things got a lot

easier for him."

"Yes, but I don't want you to miss the process. You will have setbacks and regrets before you can thwart advances in bullet time. I don't want you to get blindsided."

"And I appreciate that in you, Doc. So teach me."

"Did you finish your list of must-haves and preferences?"

"But of course. I have tunnel vision. Put me on an assignment and I'm going to knock it out."

"Good, then let's talk through that. So when you went through the exercise what was revealed to you in the process?"

"Hold on. I have it right here."

"No, don't read it to me."

"Now why would you have me waste my time, if we weren't going to review it?"

"Did you pinpoint qualities that you want in a man?"

"Yes."

"Did you learn anything in the process?"

"Yes. I want a lot and I need to bring a lot."

"Then how could it have been a waste of time? The intent of the assignment was to create a point of reference that keeps you centered and grounded."

"Grounded? Dude, you are speaking Swahili. English, man. Spit it to me in English."

"When you meet a guy you can make a sober-minded decision without the influence of ooey-gooey mushiness."

"Are you saying that I'm irrational and can't make logical decisions when it comes to men?"

"Yep, check a winner."

"Well, I take issue with that."

"That may be, but it doesn't make it untrue."

"Whatever."

"Tell you what; show me a relationship that has worked

for you and then I'll shut up."

"You think you know everything."

"No. A lot of stuff I don't know, but this one I do. Ready for another lesson?"

Debra harrumphed. "Yeah, sure. Go ahead."

"Any man who wants you for more than just sex will not only make you feel like a priority, but will make you a priority. A woman should never chase a man. How many deer have you seen chasing a lion? When a man wants something, nothing can keep him from it."

Doc Reed struck out with a chorus of Marvin Gaye and Tammi Terrell's *Ain't No Mountain High*. Debra joined him.

"You have a pretty nice voice, Debra."

"Why thank ya."

"Regroup. Class is still in session. Women make themselves accessible to men."

"We talking sex?"

"Yep. If a woman gives up her goody box—the ultimate gift—to a man who didn't have to work to attain it, she sells herself short. A wild tiger lives for the chase of the hunt. Its palate isn't satisfied when a zookeeper gives him food."

"Not if she only wants him to get that monkey off her back."

"I understood you to want a lasting relationship. If you're only in this for a back-blowing session, you don't need my help."

"I do. I do. I'm just saying if that's all she wants, what's the harm?"

"Go back to your notes on the three aspects of sex." He waited for Debra to flip through her notepad. "Her intent may start as just a physical act, but if she's the typical female, her heart will get involved. That takes us back to soul ties and again, the spiritual component."

136

Debra bowed her head. "This is too much. My goody box is yelling at me. I'm surprised you can't hear her through the phone. And you're telling me that even when my body craves a man, I shouldn't give in."

"Do we need to go all the way back to the basics? Woman of virtue; keeping yourself until marriage; self-respect and dignity."

"Not necessary." Debra set the phone on her lap, jerked like she was having a seizure, picked up the phone. "I need to go."

"Got to get back to work or you're tired of hearing me?"

"I need to run to the drugstore and buy some batteries."

Chapter 16

Except a Man Build a House

Debra darted in and out of traffic on Gettysburg Avenue. Her ability to avoid right turners, slow pokes and potholes did something for her. She smiled as she averted a line of cars held up by an RTA bus. Just as she crossed Hoover Avenue, she noticed a police cruiser tucked away in the parking lot of the vacated Popeye's Chicken. To avoid being detected by the radar gun aimed at her Mercedes, she took her foot off the accelerator. In an orchestrated move, she confirmed that her seatbelt was locked; put her hands at ten and two; held her breath as she passed. When she checked her rearview mirror to ensure she hadn't been caught, she noticed a black 2005 Impala in hot pursuit.

Debra's heart raced. She hadn't seen or heard from Vincent since he boinged Catherine in the bed she had since donated to the Salvation Army, and now he was following her. She moved into the left lane just short of rear-ending a Grand Prix which was turning into the plaza at Kings Highway. The gap between her and the Impala narrowed. She zoomed past Prescott and without using turn signals, switched to the right lane, dipped down Hillcrest. She whipped into the lot of 14KT Records and watched the

Impala continue up the street. She checked the license plates as the car sped by. Not Vincent.

She grabbed her cell, dialed Doc Reed. With a tremble in her voice, she said, "Doc, I panicked when I thought I saw Vincent. I'm not over him yet."

"First of all, are you okay? You sound like you're out of breath. You've been running?"

"Running from who I thought was Vincent." She swallowed hard. "I thought he was following me up the Burg."

"But it wasn't him?"

"No. He's got personalized plates that read 'Lova Boi'."

"Interesting."

"Why is it that I see more black Impalas now that we're not together than I ever saw before?"

"Because you're looking for Vincent."

"I don't want to see him."

"That's what your mouth says, but your heart wants something different."

"Do tell." She turned off the ignition. "I'm too shook up to drive."

"You never got closure from the situation. Yeah, you put him out, but you never got the opportunity to question his motives. You have unresolved issues and your heart is looking for answers."

"If I never see Vincent again, I'm okay with that. So how do I bring closure to this matter without, I repeat, without involving Vincent?"

"By having a crystal-clear understanding of what you need and want out of a relationship. As a result, you develop a peace of mind about the breakup because you realize he didn't meet your requirements. So to continue to invest mental, emotional and physical energy into him is a waste of time."

And money. "You make it sound easy."

"Developing this awareness gradually helps you resolve within yourself that the situation was toxic and not in your best interest."

Debra squealed.

"What's wrong?"

"Jarrus is calling! What to do? What to do?"

"Calm down, breathe and take the call."

"Okay, I'll call you back later." She picked up the call. "Good afternoon, Debra Hampton."

"Hey, Debra. This is Jarrus."

"Hi, Jarrus. How are you?"

"Well. Busy, but well. First, let me apologize for taking so long to call you."

It has been way too long. "What's it been, a couple of days?"

"More like a couple of weeks."

"Wow, time sure flies."

"Between my job and business, I've been tied up. I wanted to make sure that I had ample time to chat with you and give you my undivided attention."

Debra smiled wide, then relaxed her face so that her excitement didn't resonate through the phone. "Well, I appreciate the consideration."

"So are you ready to make good on the wager you lost?"

"Wager?" She paused for dramatic effect, snapped her fingers. "Oh yeah, you guessed my weight and owe me dinner."

"Can't beat those odds." He laughed. "So how about Saturday? Will you grant me the honor of joining me for dinner and stimulating conversation?"

"That sounds wonderful, but I need to confirm my

schedule first. Can I call you back?"

"Sure. I'll be waiting to hear from you. Have a great rest of your day."

"Same to you. Bye." Debra cranked up the air conditioner to evaporate the sweat that had formed on her forehead, palms and chest. She called Doc Reed.

"Okay, Doc. I'm back."

"What's that noise in the background?"

"Oh, my A/C." She turned off the system. "That better?"

"Much. So how'd it go?"

"He wants to take me out Saturday! I'm so excited!"

"It's good that he wants to take you out—"

"Okay, I'll call him and let him know we are on for Saturday."

"No, no, no. Oh, Lord, how long must I suffer?"

"What's that supposed to mean?"

"You haven't heard from him in a few days."

"Eighteen to be exact."

"And as soon as you hear from him, you're ready to jump in at warp speed."

"What's wrong with that? I've been waiting for him to call."

"Hunter."

"Ah, yes. The hunter wants to pursue the prey."

"Exactly. You don't want to call him now."

Debra expelled an extended, embellished sigh.

"He may be a great guy, a phenomenal guy even, but you have to assume that all he wants is your goody box."

"I'm so not into playing games."

"Play or g—"

"Get played."

"Very good, Grasshopper. Pace yourself."

"I want to call him right now."

"Now you understand that I will spend your money whether you follow my advice or not, right? Call him if you want to, but I'd wait a day before calling him."

"Dang! A day?"

"Yep."

"So tomorrow at," she looked at the clock on her car stereo, "four-thirty-two I can let him know it's a go?"

"You're special, but yes."

"As long as I'm not short-yellow-bus special."

"Have fun on your date."

"I plan on having a lot of fun." Debra lowered her voice, said, "Perrrrrrrrrrrrrrfect."

"Did you purr?"

"You heard that?"

"This date is at the foundation-building stage. If you want to frame up this house, you have to lay the foundation properly."

"Here we go."

"You want this medicine to curb your cravings, addict?"

"Okay, give it to me."

"Straight, no chaser. Take this time to share information: history, likes, dislikes. Quit trying to rush the process."

"I'm just excited, that's all. Can't you just be happy for me?"

"I am happy for you, but I don't want you to fall short of the glory."

"The glory?"

"To find, attract and marry your soul mate."

"Ouch."

"It's okay to be excited that he called, but it's just a phone call, nothing more."

"Not yet."

"Well, if you give him this energy, I don't want to think

about what he'll get if he treats you with a little respect and dignity."

"And we've come full circle to the goody box."

"For him, that's what it's all about. If you want more than a romp, then this phase has to last awhile. You cannot cloud it with sexual energy. If you speed through this stage and jump right into intimacy, the house will fall."

"No foundation?"

"No foundation."

"You sure know how to kill a high."

"My job is to tell you the truth. Look at all those poor souls on *American Idol* who've been told by family and friends that they can sing. They believe the hype and then make complete idiots of themselves on national television. I'm trying to save you the heartache and embarrassment."

"All right. I'm listening."

"After the date, you go your way and he goes his."

"I'll invite him in for coffee. Nothing more."

"No, Lord. You can invite him in if you want to, but it can go all wrong."

"Don't invite him in?"

"Nope."

"Why not? I'm a grown woman."

"If you don't invite him in, I guarantee you'll have a second date. He'll be curious to know more about this mysterious, *virtuous* woman."

"What about a kiss?"

"Not a kiss or a peck."

Chapter 17

Revolving Romance

Jarrus rang the doorbell. Not wanting to appear anxious, Debra counted to twenty before opening the door.

"Hi, Jarrus."

"Hi, beautiful." He handed her a box of Esther Price milk-chocolate candy and an Annie Lee figurine.

"Oh, Jarrus. This is so sweet."

"Thought I'd give you something other than the usual flowers."

"Thank you." She admired the figurine of a man and woman enjoying each other's company.

"It's *White Tie Only—Scene One*. A reminder of our first date."

"That's thoughtful." She walked into the living room, rearranged the centerpiece on the sofa table, set the figurine on it. "Perfect."

Jarrus smiled. "Better get going. We have reservations for six."

Debra grabbed her purse, walked to the door. "Where are we going?"

"Dinner."

"Duh. Where will we be eating dinner?"

"A restaurant."

"Okay, so you want to surprise me, I get it. Am I dressed okay?"

He stepped back to gaze at Debra. The colorful knee-length dress complemented her vibrant skin. His lengthy stare made her feel a little uncomfortable.

"Hello?"

"Oh, yeah. You are dressed just right." He put his arm around her waist, escorted her out the door.

The ride down I-75 south was relaxing and refreshing. As Doc Reed instructed, Debra kept the inquisition light.

As they passed the new Cincinnati Premium Outlets near Traders World, Jarrus said, "Have you shopped there yet?"

"No, but it's on my to-do list."

When they arrived at Radisson Hotel Cincinnati Riverfront, Jarrus opened the car door for Debra. The side split caused her dress to reveal the splendor of her petite, yet muscular legs.

Jarrus enjoyed the scenery. "Beautiful."

"It sure is." Debra looked up toward the top floor of the eighteen story hotel. "I've heard that revolving restaurant is phenomenal. I've always wanted to eat here." She looked at Jarrus. "Have you eaten here before?"

"Never. I'm a virgin." He chuckled.

Debra didn't.

Jarrus terminated the smile. "I wanted my first experience at 360 to be with you."

She smiled.

"Let's go. The gourmet chef is awaiting our arrival."

Once seated, the conversation continued.

Debra said, "How'd you know about this place?"

"I Googled it. It's one of the Top 100 Romantic

Restaurants in the United States."

"I'm sure that has a lot to do with the view. It's beautiful up here." She peered out the panoramic window.

"It takes about an hour for the restaurant to revolve one time, hence its name: 360. Before dinner is over, we'll see downtown Cincinnati, the wooded hills of northern Kentucky and the majestic Ohio River."

"You sound like an advertisement."

"I memorized the info from the site." Jarrus presented a modest smile. "Wanted to impress you."

"You've succeeded."

After dinner, they walked along the Newport Levee. A plethora of restaurants, venues for entertainment and clothing shops lined the strip. Debra spotted Cold Stone Creamery.

She pointed. "I know that I don't need it, but—"

"Your wish is my command." He took Debra by the hand and led her to the place of ice-cream pleasure.

She ordered her usual: a "love it" portion of the founder's favorite with sweet cream ice cream, brownie, pecans, fudge and caramel. "O-M-G! This is delicious. How's yours?"

"Great." He took a lick of chocolate ice cream.

Debra stared at his ability to work his tongue without losing a drop of decadent yumminess. When she noticed him noticing her, she stuffed a spoonful of ice cream into her mouth. As she licked the fudge off the spoon, she said, "I'm having a wonderful time. What's next on the agenda?"

"Thought we could go to Embassy Suites."

Debra choked on a brownie chunk, coughed to clear her throat.

"You okay?" He patted her on the back.

"Why are we going to Embassy Suites?" She wiped at the caramel trying to run down her chin.

"Do you trust me?"

"Until you give me a reason not to."

"Then trust that I will be a gentleman."

She looked up at Jarrus. His tender eyes spoke volumes to his sincerity. She quivered.

Jarrus took off his jacket, draped it over her shoulders. "That better?"

"Yes, thanks. Between the ice cream and the breeze off the water, I knew that was coming."

Jarrus put his arm around her, pulled her in close, escorted her to the Embassy Suites Atrium. They sat on a love seat and listened to an accomplished pianist tickle the keys of a black baby grand. They had great first-date conversation complete with getting-to-know-more-about-you information including likes and dislikes, kids, previous relationships, goals and aspirations.

"Why is a beautiful Black woman like you by herself?"

"Just haven't met the right guy."

Jarrus tilted his head like the RCA Victor dog and grunted like Tim "The Tool Man" Taylor from the 1990s sitcom *Home Improvement.*

Debra touched his knee "Present company excluded." She smiled. "What about you, Mr. Handsome Eligible Bachelor? Why are you unattached?"

"Just can't seem to find a compatible woman."

Debra shook her head. "You ain't said nothing."

"I don't want the night to end, but I have a full day tomorrow."

"You have to go to work?"

"No, Sunday School and since I drive the church van, my day starts at six."

"Well, I guess we better get going then."

Jarrus offered his hand.

Debra obliged him and then stood.

He kissed the back of her hand.

She blushed, dropped a coy smile.

He bent his arm at the elbow and they walked arm-in-arm to the car.

The ride home provided an additional opportunity for probing into the motive of Jarrus. Debra found herself staring at his full lips on several occasions. To stay focused, she revisited Doc Reed's words, "You can invite him in if you want to, but it can go all wrong."

Debra said, "The figurine is a great representation of our date. I had a wonderful time."

"Yeah, so did I."

He walked her to the door, lingered there.

Debra fumbled with the key. His thick chest inches from her. On the third attempt, she unlocked the door, cracked it open, looked at Jarrus, leaned toward him. Her goody box was on red alert. She toyed with circumventing Doc Reed's advice. *What harm can be done with one kiss?* She recalled that Judas betrayed Jesus with a kiss.

"You better get going. Sunday School awaits." She withdrew from his personal space, smiled. "I really appreciate the great evening, Jarrus. Thanks."

"Good night, lady."

Debra walked inside. She slowly closed the door, hoping that Jarrus would ask to stay for coffee. As the opening between the door and the frame narrowed, she watched Jarrus drive away. She closed the door, rested her forehead against it. After a moment of silence, she called Doc Reed.

"So how do you feel?"

"Awful and good. I wanted to invite him in, but at the same time I'm proud of myself for doing something different."

"And I'm proud of you. I knew you could do it."

"Empowering."

"Exactly. Change is not easy, but if your objective is the picket fence...."

"Right."

"Did you talk about the next date?"

"No. I had to get him out of here with a quickness. I didn't want to chance it. You remember how your mother would give you the if-you-show-out-in-public-I-will-embarrass-you-in-public speech before going to the grocery store?"

"Yeah."

"I had a similar conversation with my goody box before the date and I didn't want to wear out my welcome."

He chuckled. "Whatever it takes. So you know the drill, right? If he's interested, he'll call."

"You mean I still can't call him? We had a great first date."

"Uh huh."

"He made the first move, so why can't I call him just to let him know that I'm interested?"

"Do you think he doesn't realize that you're interested? If *he's* interested, he'll call in a day or so."

"But it took him almost three weeks for the first call."

"He explained that."

"But if he doesn't—"

"He may play a little cat-and-mouse thing just to shake you up, but I wouldn't worry about it. I'm telling you, he'll call." Perceiving the vulnerable state of his successful-dater-in-training, Doc Reed proceeded with a hunter-preparedness session. "Got some more info for you. Do you want to call me back or are you ready?"

"Give it to me now because I may not call you back."

"You know that if you didn't, I'd call you back, right?"

"You are relentless."

"I prefer committed, focused, goal-oriented, driven."

"Okay, Mr. Thesaurus. Can we get on with this? You are killing me."

"All right. I'll make this quick. Men can be classified into four categories of hunters: predators, ambushers, parasites and companions. The predators are like sharks that actively pursue the prey. Eat it up whole and alive. Sharks can detect a victim from miles away just by a drop of blood."

"What does the *Animal Kingdom* have to do with my date, Dr. Jacques Cousteau?"

"Focus. Focus. Sharks can hone in on wounded prey just as predator men can detect a broken or wounded heart. They are looking for an easy kill aka quick access to the goody box without much effort."

"Hmmm."

"A shark will make several passes and then the next thing you know, only your bikini bottoms are floating on the surface of the water."

"Oh my."

"Exactly. The act of predation can be broken down into four stages: detection of prey, attack, capture and consumption."

"A bit gory isn't it?"

"Yep, like severed limbs in *Jaws 1, 2* and *3*; a predator doesn't care how it leaves its victim as long as he gets what he wants."

"A full stomach?"

"Empty sperm sack."

"Geezo."

"Ambushers lie in wait, adapt to the surroundings. They are camouflaged, hiding motionless waiting for prey to come within striking distance. They use stealth and cunning versus speed or strength to outwit prey. These men come in through the backdoor to overtake their victims."

"How do you mean?"

"I used to be an ambusher."

"Get out of here! Doc, you were a hunter?"

"I sure was. I never considered myself a pretty boy so I wasn't confident with the direct approach. However, I knew that I was a good communicator and I could make women laugh. So I came in through the backdoor; acted like we were great buddies. Once I felt she trusted and confided in me, I made my move. She never knew what hit her."

"Wolf in sheep's clothing."

"Yep and like my buddy said, 'Even in sheep's clothing, when the wolf opens his mouth, he's still going to howl.'"

"Good one."

"Understand that I am not that man anymore."

"So you changed, huh?" She rolled her eyes, twisted her lips, sucked her teeth.

"It's possible and yes, I changed." Agitated by her doubtful tone, he continued. "Let me finish with the hunters. I'll explain my transition later. Parasites live off the host. Kill it slowly by devouring it in small chunks. That's the guy who lives in your house, eats your food, drives your car and consumes the goody box."

"Vincent."

"Enough said. The companion hunter is the guy who's truly looking to settle down with a lifelong mate. He's a loyal friend with unconditional love."

"Lassie."

"Okay, if that helps you wrap your mind around the concept."

"Sounds like the ambusher and companion are a lot

alike."

"Initially because that's the ambusher's strategy. Time sifts the genuine from the goody-box seekers."

"Time, huh?"

"It's the only true measure. No way around it unless you've mastered time travel." He laughed.

"I'm going to need you to stick to relationships and save the satire for another trainee."

Chapter 18

Only Fools Rush In

After another eventful morning getting the kids off to school, Rachel slumped at her desk. She found solace in the walls of her office, her place of power and passion.

She called her office husband. "Conrad, what are you doing for lunch today?"

"Nothing special. Figured I'd grab something from the sandwich cart and keep it moving."

"How about joining me at the Racquet Club? I'm meeting with Carrington Corp to close the deal. Since you've been so instrumental in making this happen, I wanted to invite you to the luncheon."

"I'm in. Thanks."

"No problem. Come to my office so we can discuss the particulars."

"On my way."

A few minutes later, reliable Conrad was seated with notepad in hand. Rachel admired how well he pieced together second-hand clothes to create an eccentric, yet charming vibe.

She rehearsed her presentation. Per Conrad's

recommendations, she made a couple of minor modifications to the delivery and content.

Confident that she was prepared to woo the client, Rachel said, "I have about an hour to wrap up another project. Meet me in the Kettering Tower lobby at a quarter 'til twelve."

"Will do. You want me to bring the handouts?"

"Sure." She handed him six professionally designed portfolios. "Thanks."

He walked out of the office, closed the door.

Consumed with the task at hand Rachel lost track of time, until Sylvia chimed in on the intercom.

"Ms. Nance, twenty minutes until your twelve o'clock meeting."

"Oh, shoot." She stood, grabbed her purse, exited the office. As she walked toward the elevator, she said, "Thanks yet again, Sylvia. Let Conrad know that I'm on my way."

"Done."

Rachel often scheduled meetings at the Dayton Racquet Club. The ambiance and food of the elitist restaurant impressed her clients, and it was down the street from her office. With her packed itinerary, she frequently dashed and dined. She kept a spare pair of pumps in her oversized purse, just in case she lost a heel in the sidewalk grating.

Rachel arrived at the steel and glass structure reminiscent of a Manhattan skyscraper—Dayton style—and then paused to catch her breath. Through the story-high glass wall, she saw Conrad waiting in the lobby, did a double take. *I know he didn't have that on this morning.*

Conrad had changed into a tailored navy-blue three-button classic suit with white pinstripes. He complemented the nondescript white dress shirt with a dark-red tie that had square patterns outlined in silver. He finished the look with a pair of high sheen lace-up black dress shoes.

"Okay, Conrad. I see you."

"What can I say? This meeting is important."

She nodded. "Well, I appreciate that in you."

"And I appreciate you." He pushed the elevator call button. When the doors opened, several people walked out. Conrad held his hand over the sensor so the doors didn't close, stepped aside. "After you."

"Thank you." On the ride to the top floor, Conrad's masculine scent filled the small quarters.

Rachel took in a deep, yet inconspicuous whiff. "What's the name of that cologne?"

"Rush by Gucci."

"Very nice."

The dynamic duo arrived in the private meeting room a few minutes before the clients. The projector, flip chart and podium were in place.

"Oh, great. The room is ready."

"Yeah, I called ahead to confirm that the audio-visuals were ready and the salads preset."

"And the meal?"

"It will be served promptly at twelve-fifteen "

"You are good."

He smiled and then positioned the portfolios at each table setting. "We're ready to go."

Rachel smiled. "Yes we are."

The president and three VPs from Carrington Corp arrived as planned. After lunch, Rachel and Conrad fielded all the questions, landed the deal. The agreement was signed and the healthy compensation check was forthcoming. The partners shook hands and the bigwigs departed.

Relaxing in the satisfaction, Rachel and Conrad lingered at the linen-draped table.

Rachel leaned back on the high-back chair. "That gives

me such a rush."

"Yeah, me, too."

"A few more deals like that and I'll have to hire some more folks."

"I've already started developing job descriptions for online posting."

Rachel sat up, leaned on the table. "How do you do that?"

"Do what?"

"Never mind." She relaxed in the chair, sighed. "Hey, while it's on my mind; are you good to cover for me next week while I'm in Jamaica?"

"Let's see." He scrolled through his Blackberry calendar. "Payroll? Check. Accounts Payable? Check. Accounts Receivable? Check. Inventory? Check. Staffing? Check." He looked up at Rachel. "I believe that's everything."

"I believe that you're right. I can relax and enjoy this trip knowing that you have it all under control." She exhaled. "The first time in a long time I've felt so at ease." She sat forward. "Thanks."

"I got you."

She smiled, redirected the conversation. "So what's going on with Syndi?"

"She decided that she's not ready to get married."

"Well, don't worry. You're a great guy. She'll come around and realize that you're the best thing for her."

"I doubt it."

"What? That you're the best thing for her?"

"Nah, that she'll come around. She's not the marrying type."

"And you didn't know that before you proposed?"

"According to her, she didn't realize until I did."

"Wow. That's amazing."

"How so?"

"Here you are wanting to get married and I'm struggling in mine."

"So how's that going for you?"

"Not well. I'm in a funky place." She stared at the ceiling. "Here I am a certified problem solver and I can't resolve this matter. It's overwhelming to say the least."

"Maybe you two should take a trip. You know, go to a neutral environment away from the demands of work and family. I heard that can rejuvenate dying love."

"I thought about it, but I'm so hurt right now, I wouldn't be good company."

"So you're going out with your girls instead?"

"But of course. All the pleasure, none of the expectations."

He crinkled his forehead.

"Sex, dude. I don't have to put out."

"Gotcha."

She looked at her watch. "Oh, man. I have another meeting in fifteen minutes."

"I had Sylvia reschedule it from two to three."

Rachel smiled and then giggled. "Wonderful, I don't have to sprint back." She stretched. "Coming off the high. My body is starting to shut down." She started to move the chair back.

"Let me get that for you." Conrad stood, pulled out the chair.

"Thank you."

She knelt to pick her purse up from the floor. As she used the table edge for stability, Conrad was retrieving his phone. Albeit brief, his hand brushed hers, their eyes met. His intimate gaze scanned her eyes, romanced her face, caressed her hair.

Rachel's pupils dilated and watered slightly for a clear

view of the life-sized sculpture standing in front of her. Moisture formed on her hands, forehead and other places— something she hadn't experienced in a long time. She touched her chest to steady the arrhythmia. She fixed her eyes on him as she slowly stood.

Conrad said, "We better get going then."

"Yeah."

They walked back to the office in silence.

~ ~ ~ ~ ~ ~ ~

The next day, Conrad knocked on Rachel's office door which was wide open.

"Do you have a minute?"

"Sure. Come in."

He entered the office, closed the door. "I know you prefer that the door remain open, but I need to discuss something confidential with you."

"Okay." She read the concern etched on his face. "Is everything all right?"

"Yeah, everything's fine." He pulled a chair close to Rachel's desk, sat, rubbed his hands together.

"Conrad, what's going on? I'm a little concerned. Never known you to be at a loss for words." She gave him a side glance. "You're leaving me, too?"

"No, nothing like that. I love my job and...."

Rachel got up from behind her desk, sat in the chair next to Conrad. With soft eyes, she said, "Tell me what's wrong."

"Something happened yesterday and I'm not sure how to process it."

"What happened?"

"Well, when we were at the business meeting...." He lowered his head.

"Yes."

"I went home and tried to shake it off. I didn't know what

to do with it or how to handle it. I'm not telling you for you to respond but...." He lifted his head.

Rachel placed her hand on her knee.

"I don't know. I've never been in this situation before."

"What are you talking about, Conrad?"

"I'm just saying...."

"What are you trying to say, man? Spit it out."

"I thought a lot about you today."

"As you should. We have a lot to get done before I jet to Jamaica."

"No, I mean I thought about *you* today." He looked into her eyes. "I can only speak for myself, but when our hands touched yesterday, I felt something." He rubbed his thighs.

Rachel felt a tug on her heart. "I guess I would be lying, and maybe I've already lied to myself, but I felt something, too."

"I don't mean to complicate your already complex life, but I had to let you know that I think I've developed feelings for you." He paused, swallowed hard. "And I don't know what to do about it."

Chapter 19

Party Line

A week after the date of her life, Debra still hadn't heard from Jarrus. Reclined on her chaise lounge in the "Me Time" room, she sipped hot tea, looked out the window. The serenity of the wooded lot allowed her to think without clouded judgment or distractions.

"Even if he never calls again, I'll be okay." She picked up *Manna for Mamma: Wisdom for Women in the Wilderness* by Dr. Vivi Monroe Congress, flipped to the chapter on *Wandering and Wondering*, read for inspiration.

As she finished the chapter and set down the book, the phone rang.

"Hello?"

"Hey, Debra. How are you?"

"I'm good." She looked at the receiver to see who was calling. "Oh, hey, Jarrus."

"Recognized my voice, huh?"

"Nope, caller ID."

"Ouch. So what've you been up to lately?"

"Ripping and running. Keeping busy. You?"

"The same. I had a great time last week."

"Yeah, me, too."

"Ready to do it again?"

"Sure."

"Great. I have tickets to Tyler Perry's play next week. Thought we could do that and dinner."

Debra frowned. "Aw, I would love to go, but I'll be in Jamaica with my girls next week."

With a hint of disappointment, he said, "Oh, that sounds nice."

"We're celebrating our liberation."

"From?"

"Management, marriage and men."

"Hmm."

"What?" She paused. "Ewwww. No, I don't play for that team. I love men, just looking to enjoy a weekend where they are not the focus of attention or conversation."

"It's like that?"

"Please don't take it personally. You've been my muse to," she threw her Black-power fist in the air, "keep hope alive."

"I was really looking forward to having you on my arm."

"What as a trophy chick?"

"Not at all. I like your company and you're beautiful. I'm a winner all the way around."

"That's so sweet. How about we connect when I get back?"

"You sure you're going to have time for me?"

"Now don't be like that."

"What about this week?"

"No can do. I have tons of loose ends that need tying," she transitioned into a Caribbean accent, "before I vacate to de island, mon. Me have tree suitcases to pack." She clapped her hands twice. In her Ohio dialect, said, "Oh, I have to get my bikini out of the cedar chest and let it air out."

"Now you're tormenting me."

"Not at all. I'm just excited about the trip. I haven't been on a vacation in yea—" The call-waiting tone interrupted. "Hold on a second, Jarrus. Got a call on the other line." She clicked over. "Hello?"

Rachel and Sherry chorused, "Hey, lady."

"My girls." She beamed. "Jarrus is on the other line."

Sherry said, "You want us to call you later?"

"Nope, I'll be right back." She clicked back to Jarrus. "Jarrus?"

"Yeah."

"That's Rachel and Sherry. We're finalizing the travel details so I need to take the call."

"Okay, can we at least set a time for our next date before you go international?"

"Sure. How about two weeks from Saturday?"

"Two weeks? Good Lord. That's the earliest you can fit me in?"

"I already know that when I get back, my desk is going to be packed with dockets, contracts and God knows what else. It'll take me awhile to catch up. That work for you?"

"I guess it's going to have to work for me. What choice do you leave me?"

"Don't be like that."

"Uh huh."

"Okay, I have to go. We'll talk. Bye." She clicked over. "What makes him think I'm sitting around all day waiting on his call?"

Sherry said, "Because that's what you've been mulling about since your fantastic date."

"Just so I can do whatever he bids. Ha! He has confused me with a lifeless sistah." She smacked her hands on her hips, rocked her head, spoke with a Latin accent. "This señorita doesn't have time to waste, Papí."

Rachel said, "You need to stop and stop now. You know good and well you've been waiting for him to reach out and touch you."

"Well, I've learned enough to know that I can't let him know."

Rachel said, "What's the harm in telling someone that you like them?"

"I know me and when I put my feelings out there, everything gets cloudy. Like I walked into a fog."

Sherry said, "Been there. Done that."

The trio said, "And I ain't going back."

Debra said, "Rachel, are you going to tell us where we're staying?"

"Why? It's not like you have to leave your travel itinerary so your man can keep track of you."

"That was low."

"Now me, on the other hand; I had to leave my complete schedule with the office and Brian."

With an exaggerated sarcasm, Debra said, "So you have such a full life that you need a team of folks to keep you organized.

"Whatever."

Sherry said, "Okay ladies. Let's start this trip off right. We need to establish some rules of engagement. Rule number one: we will not discuss our men. Rule number two: we will not discuss our jobs."

Debra said, "That's not fair. Only two of us are gainfully employed."

"What is up with you two today?

"I'm on my period. Forgive me."

Sherry shifted her eyes, tightened her jaw. "And?"

"You know how emotional I get."

"Let me tell you something, if the spirit is subject to the prophet, then the period is too."

"Humph. You took it there."

"Sure did. You're using your period to justify misplaced aggression. I'm not in that line so check that at the airplane door."

"Okay, okay." Debra expelled an extended sigh.

Rachel chuckled.

Sherry continued, "And rule number three: what happens in Jamaica...." She paused for a unanimous consensus. "Let me repeat, what happens in Jamaica...."

"Stays in Jamaica."

Chapter 20

Island Adventure

Debra and Rachel rode together to Cox International Airport. The flashing marquee indicated that the threat level was orange.

Rachel said, "I'm glad we got here early. The gate agents are on high alert today." She looked at Debra. "Did you put your toiletries in your carry-on or the luggage you're going to check?"

"In my check bag, but if I switch it, maybe I'll get singled out for a strip search."

"They do not do cavity searches, pervert."

"Oh, well that's disappointing." Debra parked in the long-term lot.

As they stepped onto the shuttle bus, Rachel said, "So how's it going with Jarrus?"

"It's going okay."

"You should've let him drop us off at the airport."

"Nah, he made me wait, so now it's his turn."

"Sounds so manipulative."

"I'm not trying to manipulate him. I'm trying to control my emotions and avoid my usual knee-jerk reactions.

165

Waiting for his heart to align with mine."

"Those are not your words."

"Well, I can't take credit for them, but I'm going to live by them. I like the way I feel."

"Hearts aligning reminds me of," Rachel waved her hand in the air like Merlin the Magician, "the alignment of the stars." She expelled a haunting howl, handed the driver a tip, stepped off the shuttle.

"Girl, bye. This is not hocus pocus, voodoo or Madam Cleo. The only person I'm manipulating is me. I'm doing me, but in a different way. You should be happy for me. I haven't cried on your shoulder or called you for a drive-by."

"Whatever." Rachel looked at the clock on the wall. "Sherry better hurry up or she's going to celebrate her pseudo retirement in Dayton."

"Is this place for adults only? I'm not trying to deal with hollering kids and frustrated parents."

"What's that supposed to mean? You trying to say that my kids are unruly?"

"What in the world? I'm just saying. I haven't been on a vacation in a long time and since you won't disclose our lodging arrangements," she slid the Havana brown Prada sunglasses down the bridge of her nose, looked over the top, "I have to ask these probing questions."

"Why are you wearing those inside the airport?"

"Honey, I started my vacation when I left the house." She let the strap of her Louis Vuitton purse slide from her shoulder to the crook of her arm and swing.

"You're a mess."

"And this mess is about to have a blast. Where's my Bahama Mama?"

"We're going to Montego Bay, not Nassau."

"Okay, then, my Rum Punch."

"Awful. You got your passport?"

"Yes, mother dear." She saw Sherry standing near the sliding doors and then called out to her. "Hey lady, we were getting a little concerned."

"Sorry about that. Took me a minute to say my good-byes to Dwight."

Rachel and Debra looked around the lobby searching for a likely candidate. They came up empty.

Debra said, "Where is he?"

"Yeah, we want to meet this mysterious lova man."

"He just pulled off."

Rachel said, "Sure he did. Why didn't he bring in your bags?"

"He did bring them in." She pointed to the three bags staged near the AirTran check-in station.

"How'd we miss him?"

Sherry shrugged. "I'm so excited about our excursion." She looked at Debra. "Did she divulge where we're staying?"

With pouted lips, Debra said, "Get real."

After an uneventful non-stop flight, the plane touched down at the Sangster International Airport.

Debra said, "MoBay, here we come!"

Sherry said, "The average temperature is eighty degrees during the day and around seventy at night. Once notorious for the buccaneers and swashbuckling pirates who made the island their home over three hundred years ago, the island is the heart of the Caribbean. It's famous for the unique appeal of its scenic and rugged interior combined with the unmatched beauty of dazzling tropical beaches bordering the blue-green water of the Caribbean Sea."

"I need you to take off your analytical hat and enjoy this beautiful tropical island," Debra said, as she strutted down the jet way to the gate.

Five men dressed in festive garb played steel drums and sang. They nodded to greet the travelers as they emerged from the plane.

Sherry said, "Karl Folkes believes that the language referred to as 'Patois' should be officially labeled 'Jamaican Creole' or just 'Jamaican'."

Debra took off her glasses, glared at Sherry.

"You know that I had to research it."

"You should have left that at the DYT." She twirled around in two complete circles; arms spanned wide. "I'm loving this place."

After they processed through immigration, Sherry pointed to a uniformed native islander. "Rachel, he's got a sign with your name on it."

"Great. I was looking for him."

"What in the world?"

"Let's go, ladies. Now the fun begins."

Debra and Sherry followed Rachel to the sign-holding man. She spoke in a low voice so that her girls couldn't hear.

The man waved over a skycap who moved expeditiously with cart in tow.

Sherry said, "Oh, I'm getting my own bags. This girl is on a serious budget."

Rachel sneered at her. "If you don't let me do this my way. Everything's been taken care of. Put your money and your inhibitions away."

Sherry and Debra looked at each other with eyebrows raised, mouths open.

Sherry said, "You don't have to tell me twice." She stepped aside so the gentleman could retrieve her carry-on bag. "Let's do this." She looked at Rachel, nodded toward the man.

"I got that, too." She reached into her purse, pulled out a bank envelope with "Tips" written on it, waved it in Sherry's face.

"Okay, I get it." She adjusted her fanny pack, put on a straw hat, cocked it to the side.

Debra said, "The hat is cute, but that kangaroo pouch has to go. Makes you look like our grandmother." She tugged at Sherry's waist. "Off with it. Right now!"

Rachel said, "Dwight let you out of the house with that on?"

"I put it on in the plane."

"Come on, Moms Mabley."

"Whatever."

The trio followed the skycap to baggage claim and then ground transportation. Waiting at the curb was a white, eight-passenger Lincoln Town Car limousine. The chauffeur was dressed in a black suit, white gloves, a captain's hat and shades. As the ladies approached, he opened the rear door, offered his hand to assist his passengers into the elegant vehicle.

Rachel said, "Ladies, your carriage awaits "

"OMG!" Debra squealed as she peeked inside the limo. "It's got everything: TV, lights, pillows and mirrors on the ceiling. Freaky!"

Sherry bumped her with her hip. "Get in so we can all enjoy the view."

Rachel shook her head. "I can take the woman out of the ghetto, but...."

Sherry said, "I heard that."

"Oh, did I say that out loud?"

"Funny. Not!"

Debra said, "What's in the bar?"

Rachel said, "Fifteen minutes and we'll be at our hotel.

Think you can wait that long?"

"IDK as Aisha would say."

"You have issues."

"As do you." She smiled. "I just love our banter, Rachel. Gives me energy for some weird reason."

"Because you're weird."

"I know you are, but what am I?"

"Oh, Lord."

"Twinkle twinkle little star, what you say—"

Rachel looked through the sunroof of the limo. "Oh, God have mercy on this wretched child of yours and make it stop!"

"I'm rubber and you're glue…." Stunned by the beauty of the majestic landscape, Debra sat quietly the remainder of the ride, stared out the window.

Debra and Sherry waited as the bellhop retrieved their bags from the trunk while Rachel walked to the front desk of the Rose Hall Resort Spa.

Sherry nudged Debra, whispered from the corner of her mouth, "I thought Rachel was taking care of tips."

Debra nudged her back. "She did. Her slight of hand is impressive. She had to have been a pickpocket in another life."

By the time they met Rachel in the lobby, she had the room cards in hand and pointed to the elevator.

"Girl, you have out-done yourself this time. This place is beautiful. Even the elevators are lovely."

"You ain't seen nothing yet." Rachel smirked, squared her shoulders. She held the room card in her hand. "Who wants the privilege?"

Debra snatched the card. "Uh, that would be me."

"It's my celebration." Sherry crossed her arms, pouted.

"Here, girl. Dang."

"Thanks." She raced out of the elevator and then stopped, looked back at Rachel. "What's the room number?"

"Ha! I'm not telling. Follow the bellhop."

"You carry a surprise just a little too far," Debra said, as she walked behind the trolley of baggage. "We packed like we're going to be here for a month."

The bellhop stopped at the room. The wooden placard next to the door had 'Prime Minister Suite' etched in it.

Sherry said, "What kind of room has a name and not a number?"

Debra squealed. "A luxury suite! Are you serious?" She jumped up and down, hugged Rachel. "OMG! OMG!"

"That's so aggravating."

Sherry swung open the door, her eyes widened, jaw slacked. Before her was 2,220 square feet of luxurious living. The suite had an oversized parlor with sitting and dining areas. The oceanfront view from the large windows was canopied by the Blue Mountains.

"This place is bigger than my whole apartment."

"It's about the size of my house, why you playin'?" Debra turned to Rachel. "Girl, how much is this room?"

"Don't worry about what it costs. We each have our own room and bathroom. Figured we'd let Sherry have the master. It has a private balcony."

Sherry clapped her hands, bounced like a toddler. "Oh goody, goody, goody."

Debra said, "Who's using this room?" She pointed at the kitchen. "Definitely didn't come on vacation to cook."

Sherry said, "Internet access? That's off limits. No checking e-mails."

Rachel said, "I can't commit to that one. I didn't bring my laptop, but I will probably use my phone to stay in touch with the kids and Conrad."

Sherry said, "You mean Brian?"

Rachel said, "Wait for it.... Wait for it...." She stood, cocked her head.

Debra said, "He's her office husband and has taken the liberty of granting her a pass to take off work for a few days."

"Oh."

"Stella got her groove jumped off in Dayton."

"Whatever. Conrad called in a couple of favors and voila! Paradise. So quit hatin' and start vacatin'. It's time to dip."

"Skinny dip?"

"Only you."

The friends retreated to their private quarters, changed into poolside loungewear and then reconvened in the living room.

Rachel said, "Debra, I love that swim suit. It looks great on you."

"Thank ya much." She twirled to show off the black one-piece with diamond-shaped cut-outs embellished with rhinestones and exposing chocolate flesh.

"Tell me that I am not going to have to look at your behind all week."

"It's not my fault the designer made it a thong. I've got a sheer cover-up."

"Then tell me that you are not planning to swim in it. You make one wrong move and all that is good and grand in the land of Ms. Deb will be viewable by the general public."

"You already know. This one is exhibition only, baby."

Rachel shook her head. "I'll be walking a few steps in front of you at all times."

Sherry said, "I couldn't prance around in something like that, but it does look good on you."

"Girl, bye. You have the body for it."

"Yeah, but not the nerve." She slid an oversized T-shirt over her tank-top bikini.

"You have got to be kidding me."

~ ~ ~ ~ ~ ~ ~

Relaxed in chaise lounges under the shade of white umbrellas, the ladies ordered drinks and then applied sunscreen.

Rachel said, "You girls know that I love you, right?"

They both nodded.

"Then don't take this the wrong way, but I'm not trying to spend every minute of this trip as a group. You do you and I'm going to do me. No schedule, no meeting times, no agenda. I might be partying at two in the morning while you guys sleep."

Debra said, "Or vice versa."

"Exactly. I just want to make sure that everyone gets out of this trip what they need. We all need to detox. The trick is doing it in a productive manner."

Debra said, "Or in private."

"You just be sure to keep that little lady pointed south and you'll be all right."

"Hold on now. I can get creative. Ol' girl can still be pointed south and I have a good ol' time."

"Where's the chastity belt?"

"Not going there. Just pointing out the flaw in your logic."

"Freak."

"I'm working on a celibacy record, so there." She stuck her tongue out at Rachel.

"What? Four weeks?"

"Uh, no. I've been sexless for almost five months."

"Amazing."

"I know it."

"No. Not that you've been celibate for four months."

"Almost five."

"But that it's your record."

"Whatever."

Rachel noticed a family of five playing in the pool. She sighed.

Debra said, "You miss your family?"

"I miss the kids."

"Not Brian?"

Rachel removed her sunglasses, turned to Debra. "Can I be honest with you?"

"I expect nothing less."

Sherry got up from her lounge chair, sat at Rachel's feet.

"I never got over my first love."

"Brian's not your first love?"

"No." She bowed her head, spoke in a low voice. "My first love was Donald. He was a sophomore when I was a freshman. We dated through high school and into his first year of college."

Debra and Sherry sat with mouths gaped, eyes wide.

"We had a great friendship: studied together and stayed on the dean's list, ran track so we hung out at meets. We even volunteered as peer advisors. When he went off to college, we committed to each other with a friendship ring." Rachel held up her right hand, pointed at the ring on her pinky finger. "I had it resized." Her voice trembled as she continued. "But he got to college and forgot about me."

"That's awful."

"Things were cool the first few months, but then his calls came less often and he always had an excuse for not coming home. So I made a surprise visit." She paused to regroup.

Sherry said, "You okay?"

She nodded. "I waited in the lobby of his dorm. About an hour later, he walked in the building hugged up with a female."

Debra said, "Get out of here."

"That's not the worst of it. She was pregnant."

Sherry flung her hand over her mouth.

Debra shook her head.

"He apologized for not telling me."

"Oh, not for playing hide Mr. Johnson in the skank's cootie."

Rachel shook her head. "Then he walked away with his arm around her like I never existed to him."

"Are you serious?"

"Very much so."

"You ever hear from him again?"

"Not until I saw their wedding announcement in *Jet*."

Debra said, "Your wedding picture was in *Jet*, too."

"Yeah, I was hoping that he'd see that I moved on like he did."

"I had no idea."

"Between him and my father not being around, I have emptiness in my heart that Brian can never fill."

"What do you mean your father? Mr. Nance is your dad, right?"

"He's my dad and a great man, but he's not my biological father. My father left us when I was three."

Debra said, "You really know how to drop nuggets."

"Didn't mean to bring you down, but I've been doing a lot of introspection lately and I know those unresolved hurts are keeping me from totally loving Brian."

"Wow."

"Now don't get it wrong, he's done enough things on his own to tick me off, but he's trying to peel away the years of hurt."

Debra said, "Sounds like you need to talk with D—"

"Oh, Lord! Next subject."

"I'm serious, Rachel."

"I don't need him. I just need to cut loose. Be free."

"Free of what?"

"Free of me. My thoughts and actions are so contrary to who I've always been. I'm not sure if I am who I am because of life situations or if the brazen female who had been subverted for years, finally broke through."

"Brazen? What are you talking about? You've been creeping?"

"No, nothing like that, but I'd be lying if I said I hadn't thought about it. I am at my sexual peak, but I don't want to have sex with Brian."

"That emotional baggage is a heavy weight to bear."

"You're telling me."

Debra said, "So how do you let it go and move on?"

"I don't know. If I did, I'd have this worked out already."

Sherry said, "Girl, you just have to trust that the Lord will make it better."

"Thanks, Sherry. But you know I'm not the water walker. I'll cheer you on all day long, but from the safety and security of the boat." She shook her head. "I have two character flaws."

Debra said, "Only two?"

Sherry nudged her, rubbed Rachel's lower legs.

"I'm a problem solver, not a faith walker."

Sherry said, "We all have growing to do when it comes to our walk with God. I'm just getting to the place where I tell Him, 'Lord, if You don't do it, it won't get done.'"

"Yeah, but what do you do when you don't want to pray? I know the Scriptures, love the Lord, still go to church every Sunday. But when I understood why I felt the way I did about Brian and realized the selfish motive behind many of my decisions, I got angry: angry at myself, angry at Brian, angry at God." Tears flowed. "I got quiet on God."

"So just get back to talking to Him. Make time to pray, re-establish that relationship."

"And thus, character flaw number two. I'm loyal to a fault. Will do anything and everything I can to help those closest to me succeed: time, money, referrals. Anything I have I make available."

Sherry and Debra nodded in agreement.

"But once you violate my trust or hurt me, then I'm done. I shut it down and shut you out. At times, I can almost feel a wall being constructed around my heart. I compartmentalize that person into the fool-me-once-shame-on-you room and never let them out."

Sherry said, "I would have never known."

"That's because I'm so guarded I don't let many people into that space."

Debra said, "I'm glad that you let us in."

"You two snuck in when I was focused on my undergraduate studies." She looked at her friends, smiled. "But you are my girls and I love you like sisters."

They hugged.

Rachel continued to vent. "I feel betrayed by God. How could He let me get into this mess? Donald, my father, Brian. Even the situation with Bob trying to sabotage my company bothered me more than I let on. Not only was he a co-worker, but he was a trusted friend. He played me for all my information and resources and just when he figured he had enough to launch out on his own, he bailed. If it weren't for

Conrad, RJ Nance Marketing may have been totally wiped out." She wiped at the tears. "The men in my life keep letting me down and I don't know that I like who I am anymore."

Sherry said, "You can't let the actions of men affect your self-esteem."

Rachel sat up. "Are you serious? Most of the hell that we've experienced has been because of men. And more specifically, the men *we* chose. Other than my father, I picked every man who wreaked havoc in my life and took a wrecking ball to my heart. It's my fault all right." She poked herself in the chest. "I blame me and," she pointed to the sky, "Him."

"Wow."

"Just being honest. And until I can get back to where I'm talking to the Lord, I'll continue to march around this mountain. It's such an awful place."

Debra sat up, swung her legs around, sat on the side of her chair. "So what can we do to help?"

"Just keep being my girls. Loving me, listening to me, encouraging me. Other than that, the rest is on me."

Debra said, "We got you, girl."

Sherry said, "I know that's right. You can depend on us."

"I knew that I could."

Debra's countenance saddened.

Rachel said, "What's wrong?"

"I feel bad that you've been carrying this burden all by yourself for all these years."

"Don't feel bad, girl. I'm just putting the pieces of the puzzle together myself."

Sherry raised her bottle of Evian water. "I say that we commit to lifelong sisterhood."

"Here. Here." They clanked their beverages together.

Sherry said, "We should have a name for our sisterhood."

Debra overheard the lady next to her place a drink order. "Sex on the Beach Girls?"

Rachel said, "That's a negative."

Sherry said, "You ever done it on the beach?"

Debra said, "I had the chance once, but he chickened out."

"Really? Why?"

"It was broad daylight and the beach was crowded."

Sherry shook her head.

"What? I have to make that happen one day."

Rachel said, "You can fool around on the beach if you want. You'll find sand for weeks to come. Believe me, I know."

Debra said, "Okay, Rachel. You have gotten a little wear and tear on that goody box, huh?"

Sherry said, "That's it! The Goody Box Girls!"

"I love it."

Rachel mumbled, put her index finger to her cheek. "Yeah, I like, I like."

Debra said, "I heard that the outdoor massages have been known to make you have an orgasm. Either of you interested in scheduling a one-hour session or two or three?"

~ ~ ~ ~ ~ ~ ~

For the rest of the trip, the Goody Box Girls vacated the cares of home and lived in the moment. They went on several excursions including swimming with dolphins and climbing Dunns River Falls in Ocho Rios. They enjoyed the clear waters on jet skis, snorkeling and an aerial view by parasail. They purchased souvenirs and swapped trinkets at the straw market. They rode motor bikes—on the "wrong side" of the street—to the nude beach in Negril. Although each had sworn to walk the beach in her birthday suit, they collectively decided that spectators didn't have to worry about photos appearing on cyberspace years later. The girlfriends opted instead to stroll the beach in swim suits: Rachel and Debra in bikinis, Sherry in a one-piece with an oversized scarf as a cover-up.

Chapter 21

Early to Rise

Rachel was always the first to arrive at the office. The workday started at nine o'clock for her employees, but she tried to get there before eight. The extra time allowed her to unwind from the get-the-kids-off-to-school frenzy and gear up for the hectic pace of making money by helping clients make money.

She turned on her laptop, logged onto Pandora.com and selected the station she customized with Gerald Levert, Jaheim and Trey Songz.

About fifteen minutes after she settled behind her desk, a tap on the door startled her. She knocked the phone off the desk. "Just a minute." She picked up the phone, walked to the door, opened it.

She released a sigh of relief. "Oh, Conrad. What are you doing here so early?"

"Had a few things to wrap up. Didn't mean to startle you. Sorry."

"You're okay. I'm just not used to anyone else being here."

"I saw that your light was on. May I come in for a

moment?"

"Sure." She stepped aside to let Conrad walk past her. His morning-fresh scent intoxicated her momentarily. In her stupor, she closed the door. "So what's on your mind?"

"I need your feedback on the Swanson project."

"What do you want to know?"

"I'm having a little trouble reading him. He seems...."

"Weird."

"Yeah, very much so."

"Yep, that's Mr. Swanson. Not to worry, he's a great person and a profound businessman. I've learned a lot from him. Just let him set the pace of the meetings and the project. He knows what he wants; it just takes him awhile to communicate it. And if you try to rush him through it, he will let you know with a quickness that *he* is the client." She chuckled.

"Well, that's good to know."

"You passed the test."

"The what?"

"Test." She noticed Conrad's confusion, continued. "I knew that Mr. Swanson would be a bit difficult."

"A bit? He's special."

"Yeah, he is, but I also knew that you could handle his specialness and you did. Mr. Swanson called yesterday to tell me that he liked working with you."

"Really? He didn't seem to care much for me."

"That's his way. He's also a proctor."

"Always the student. You just never know who's watching."

"Learning and teaching go hand in hand. As Lao Tzu said, 'Give a man a fish feed him for a day.'"

Conrad said, "'Teach a man to fish and feed him for a lifetime.'"

"Okay, philosopher. I see you."

Conrad noticed a framed picture of the Monroe family setting on Rachel's desk. In the non-traditional pose, Rachel and Brian were sitting back-to-back on a bright-white floor. The children stood behind them and the dog was lying on Rachel's lap.

"You have a beautiful family." He picked up the picture to examine it more closely.

"Thanks. This is the first professional photo we've taken in awhile."

"I don't see you as a dog owner."

"Why? Because I'm fierce at work?"

"You just don't seem like the nurturing kind."

"Actually, I'm as loving and nurturing as I am ambitious and driven. I switch uniforms on the commute home."

"And a dog? Get out of here."

"I love my Mogli. He sleeps by my side of the bed to protect me at night and he's the first to greet me in the morning. He meets me at the door when I come home, wagging his tail and jumping. I know he's saying 'Momma's home. Momma's home! He's great company during my morning walks. And I think he frowns when I leave him. Can dogs frown?"

"I'm not sure, but I don't think so." He smirked.

"Aw, this doesn't interest you. Only a dog lover can appreciate the camaraderie and unconditional love a doggy mommy shares with her baby."

"I had a dog as a child. Loved Julie with all my heart. She was a mixed-breed grey poodle."

"And no pets now?"

"If my boss wasn't such a task master who kept me away from home so much, I'd have a dog now."

"You should find yourself a new job."

"I like the company. I think I'll stay awhile longer."

She smiled. "My Mogli is precious. No back talk. No expectations except for food, water, shelter and an occasional belly rub. He's the only male who hasn't let me down. He even had my back when Brian's brother stepped to me with his fist raised."

"Say what?"

"Yeah, Mogli jumped in front of me, growled and bore all ten of his teeth." She chuckled. "He's older than my kids. I've had him for almost thirteen years. He's in great health except for his teeth. Man, I love that dog."

"No, I'm talking about your brother-in-law coming at you with his fist. Was Brian there?"

She bowed her head. "Yeah."

"Good, then he handled it."

Rachel pretended she didn't hear the statement and occupied herself by fumbling through the stack of papers in her in-box.

"He did handle it, right?"

She twisted her lip, fiddled with the papers.

"What did he do?"

"Nothing."

"Say what? He saw his brother come at you and did nothing?"

She nodded.

"There is no way I'd let a man, woman or child disrespect my queen. He would have been propped up against the wall with my hands around his neck."

"So you pack a lot of punch, huh?"

"Wouldn't have to hit him. Just post him on the wall, talk to him a little. Let him know that his behavior is unacceptable."

"Oh, so you're skilled in the office and the art of war?"

"I have many skills yet untapped."

Rachel blushed.

"I'm a third-degree black belt. Discipline keeps me from causing unjust harm, but that right there would have pushed me to the limit." He huffed to diffuse the rage.

His reaction excited Rachel. Despite her forthright business savvy she was a little girl in a woman's body. Conrad's bad-boy swag spoke volumes to her need for security.

Conrad said, "That stuff ticks me off. I made Syndi my sole focus. I protected her and gave her all of me and still came up empty." He sat on the edge of the chair, leaned forward. "I'm a good guy who's tired of being lumped into the all-men-are-dogs category. I tried to make things work with Syndi, but she refused to reciprocate my love."

"Reciprocity is the most fulfilling love. You both give unselfishly and in return, you receive all that you need." She expelled a sigh of longing. "I can't name a single couple who has that kind of commitment."

"Not even you?"

"Especially not me."

"That's disheartening. Everyone should experience a loving relationship at least once."

"It's like something is missing." Rachel touched her heart. "I can't explain it, but—"

"You don't have to. I know what you're talking about."

She looked at Conrad, noticed that he had exchanged his Clark Kent glasses for contacts. His dark-brown eyes seemed to search her soul for that small space yet untouched with hurt, pain and disappointment. She looked away when she realized that she was staring at him.

Conrad said, "How about we make a pact to help each other navigate through relationships? I'll tell you why men do what they do and you help me with women."

Rachel tapped her index finger on her cheek. "Hmmm, that might just work. Because for the life of me, I cannot figure out why Brian does the asinine things that he does. Drives me up a wall. Especially that standard I'll-get-around-to-it reply. Aaagh." She smacked her fist on the desk like a judge with his gavel.

"And I don't understand women. Tell me that you want flowers and candy and when I bring it, you say that the roses and chocolates were symbolic of what you really meant. Sorry, but I have not found the secret code to decipher the encrypted mind of a woman. To a man, flowers and candy mean flowers and candy."

"Yeah, I could've saved you some time and money on that one."

They laughed.

Conrad said, "We need each other."

"I agree."

"And we'll have each other's back."

She smiled. "I'd like that."

"Me, too."

Sylvia knocked on the door.

"Come in."

"Ms. Nance, sorry to interrupt," the inflection in her voice shifted to subtle sarcasm, "your closed-door meeting." She cleared her throat, returned to her professional voice, "But you didn't answer the intercom."

Rachel looked down at the phone. "Oh, sorry, Sylvia. I must have turned it off accidentally when I dropped the phone."

"Sherry Harris is here to see you. Should I have her wait in the lobby?"

"No, send her in."

Conrad stood as Sherry walked toward him.

Rachel said, "Sherry, this is Conrad, my office manager. Conrad, this is my girlfriend, Sherry."

They shook hands.

Conrad held Sherry's hand as she took a seat.

"Thank you, Conrad. It's a pleasure to finally meet you. Rachel spoke highly of you on our trip to Jamaica."

"Oh?"

"Yes. Thanks for keeping the place running so she could get away."

"It was my pleasure." He turned to Rachel. "Well, Ms. Nance, is there anything more we need to discuss for the project?"

"Huh? Oh, no. That'll be all, Conrad. Thanks."

"Very well. I'll leave you ladies to your business." He turned to walk away.

Rachel said, "Be sure to call me later with an update."

He looked back, nodded. "Will do."

Sherry watched Rachel who watched Conrad exit the room and close the door.

"So that's the office husband, huh?"

"Yeah."

"That guy is every bit of sexy. How do you stay focused at work with such a good-looking man around? And he's helpful, gentlemanly…." She looked at her hand. "Did you see his chivalry? He's the bomb."

"I know you didn't come here to discuss Conrad, so what's up?"

"I was considering having a dinner and wanted your input."

"What kind of dinner?"

"An I'm-ready-for-my-girls-to-meet-Dwight dinner."

"Really? I'm on board. I feel like Velma on *Scooby Doo*.

We're going ghost chasing."

"Whatever. Can we have a little get-together at your place?"

"Sure. Who are you inviting?"

"The three of us and our men."

"Party of five then. I can accommodate that."

"You are awful. Dwight is real." She narrowed her eyes, kissed the air. "Believe me."

"What's all that about? You gave up the ghost?"

"No, no goody goody for Dwight. He just makes my heart flutter."

"Humph. You're going for the Esther anointing then, huh?"

"The what?"

"Preparation for a year before you access the king."

"You know what? I have come to the conclusion that you have issues. Now I'm willing to accept that and move on because I love you nonetheless. However," Sherry pointed at Rachel, "you are not going to make me feel bad for waiting on sex. If Dwight and I are okay with it, then you should be, too."

"How do you know he's not getting his needs met by another, more accommodating female?"

"I don't. I just have to trust that he's being faithful and honoring our commitment."

"And if he's not?"

"Then he's not the one and I still come out on top. A little brokenhearted, but my virtue intact. He can get sex anywhere, but love; that's something different all together."

"Doc Reed?"

"You know it."

"Okay, what's on the menu?"

"I was thinking about a barbecue."

"I like. I like."

"Dwight loves to grill and I'll bring my world-famous mac and cheese, cabbage and dess—"

"Tell you what, I'll have it catered. That way you can spend your energy finding a Dwight and not worrying about the food."

"You are going to eat your words."

Chapter 22

Gallant Gala

Not much for socializing with co-workers on her personal time, Debra hated attending the annual appreciation gala sponsored by the firm. The list of almost five-hundred guests included clients, business leaders and city officials. Not that the folks were bouji, she just had more important things to do.

Despite the fact that she didn't want to be at the black-tie affair, she made a conscious effort to wear a memorable gown. The Monday after the event was her time to be the celebrity of the firm as everyone buzzed about how beautiful she looked. This year, she opted for a long-sleeved floor-length gown with a plunging neckline to spotlight her ample bosom. The backless evening dress came to a point just below the small of her back. She was glad that she decided against the African-violet tramp stamp. The fitted design made it difficult to take her regular stride, so she modified her gait. The smaller steps gave a little extra sway to her hips. She sashayed to the check-in table in the vestibule of the Mandalay Banquet Center.

Marcellus stood, extended his hand, said, "Good evening,

Ms. Hampton. You look absolutely radiant in that purple, the color of royalty."

"Thanks, Marcellus. You're looking quite dapper yourself."

He tugged at the collar of his tuxedo shirt. "I hate this penguin suit."

"I see we have a lot of penguins here tonight."

"Yes indeed."

"At what table am I seated?"

He ran his index finger down five sheets of guest names before finding hers. "You're at table seventeen."

"Thanks. Is that near the bar?"

"Right next to it."

"Wonderful. If you need me, you know where I'll be." She strolled into the ballroom. A mini-Philharmonic orchestra in the front corner of the room played Stevie Wonder's *Isn't She Lovely.*

How appropriate for the entrance of a queen. Debra spotted the bar, glided toward it and then stopped five feet shy of her destination. Her posture shifted from confident to insecure. Her breathing labored, her stomach cramped. The glitter in her makeup glistened brightly in the perspiration that beaded on her forehead. Vincent. Suited up, fresh haircut, looking great. She knew that he smelled wonderful. Her knees buckled.

"Pull yourself together." So as not to draw the attention of the armed hunter, she discreetly reached into her purse and pretended to look for something. She texted Doc Reed.

Ms. Deb: Vincent at gala! Help!

Doc Reed: Want me to call you?

Ms. Deb: No, not a good look with bosses & clients. I'm scared.

Doc Reed: Calm down. You can do this. He's

just a man.

Ms. Deb: What do I do?

Doc Reed: Nothing. Wait for him to approach you.

Ms. Deb: And then?

Doc Reed: Go corporate on him.

Ms. Deb: I want to go postal on him.

Doc Reed: No ma'am. Corporate. Matter-of-fact. About business. Nothing personal.

Ms. Deb: Aaagh! He's coming toward me!

Doc Reed: You got this!

Debra closed her purse, walked to the bar. She leaned on it for support so her quaking knees didn't betray her. She smiled at the bartender.

"Hi. What do you recomm—"

"Debra? Is that you?"

She inhaled, turned slowly to look into the crosshairs of the archer's bow. *He's just a man.* "Hi, Vincent." She started to turn back to the bartender, when he touched her arm. She quivered.

"Hey, girl. You look great. I'm loving the short hair."

"Thanks."

He offered her a glass of champagne. "Here, you'll love this."

"Thanks."

"So what have you been doing?"

"Working up to partner, enjoying life. You know, the usual. And you?"

"Working the room."

"And how's it going with Catherine?"

"That's over. She didn't compare to you." He touched her hand.

She stirred for a moment and then replayed Doc Reed's

words: *He's just a man.*

"I don't know what I was thinking, but I miss you and want you back. I need you," he leaned toward her, whispered, "Gumball."

No he didn't use the nickname card. The term of endearment had been his means to diffuse her outbursts in the past. She cringed at the thought of him trying to use it to manipulate his way back into her goody box.

"Well, I *know* what I'm thinking." She moved in close to Vincent, felt his breath on her lips, brushed her breasts on his forearm. "And it does not include you." She sipped the champagne, placed the glass on the serving tray, strolled away. She didn't bother to look back at Vincent, but she knew that he had a long night ahead. Because as he worked the room and offered champagne to the banquet guests, he had to balance the serving tray in his right hand and pick up his face with the left.

Chapter 23

Balance of Power

Debra loved her new home, but hated homeownership. Her mortgage was higher than when she lived in the downtown condo, but was well within her budget. What she detested was mowing the lawn, trimming shrubs and weeding the flower bed. She didn't want to be the dreaded neighbor from hell whose yard had patches of dirt in some spots and overgrown wild flowers in others, especially not in this community where only a few chocolate people resided.

Although her father taught her and her younger sister how to do "man's work"—changing a tire, replacing damaged roof shingles and gutting fresh kill—she preferred to keep her manicured hands free of calluses, dirt and debris. She had planned to contract with her uncle's lawn care company, but never got around to it. Now, halfway through mowing her half-acre property, the mower stopped.

"Frick!" Debra waited for the blade to stop moving. She added gas and then checked the spark plug and oil. When the mower didn't start, she tipped it on its side. Clumps of grass had jammed the mulch chute. She grabbed the yard gloves from the garage and commenced to removing what looked and smelled like cow manure. As she stuffed the dung in a city-provided yard bag, a white Cadillac parked in front of her house.

An attractive man stepped out of the car removing his sunglasses as he walked toward her. His biceps escaped from the wife-beater shirt. His massive calves flexed out of the khaki cargo pants. His toes waved at her through leather sandals.

"Hey, Queen. Looks like you could use a little help."

Debra stood. "Hi. Yeah, I have a mess on my hands."

He squatted to inspect the mower. "My name is Douglas, but my friends call me Doug."

"And how may I address you?" She fluttered her sweat-soaked lashes.

"Doug." He stood and set the mower back on its wheels. "Here's your problem."

"Oh, Lord. What's this going to cost me?"

"I'd say about…."

She readied herself for the bad news.

"Dinner and dancing."

Debra chuckled. "Huh?"

"Your wheels aren't adjusted to the same height. See this one here?" He pointed to a front wheel. It's higher than the other three, so it's not cutting right."

"Are you serious?"

"Yep. You're putting in a lot more work than you need to be." He adjusted the wheel. "Good as new."

"Thanks."

"Now tell me why your husband has you out here mowing this land."

"I don't have a husband."

"Your man?"

"Not one of those either."

"Your girl?"

She twisted her lips. "I don't play for that team." She leaned on her Mercedes that was parked in the driveway.

"So you're here all alone with no one to help you?"

She nodded.

"I'll swing by later and finish cutting the grass for you. I'm not dressed for the occasion." He pointed to his toes and then wiggled them.

"I appreciate that. Thanks so much."

"No problem. My folks live just down the street. I pop in every now and then to check on them. I can stop through to help you out."

"That is so nice of you, Doug. Can I get you a glass of water?"

"No, I'm good. Tell me a little about you, uh...." He walked toward her, stood next to the car.

"Oh, I'm Debra. That's so rude. Sorry. Got so caught up in the mower. I'd shake your hand, but my hands are filthy." She pulled off the yard gloves. "A little about me...." She tapped her fingers on the hood of her car. "I've been in this neighborhood for just under a year."

"Figured you hadn't been here long. No way I would've missed you." He looked her up and down. "How old are you, Deb? You mind if I call you Deb?"

"Not at all."

"Are you about thirty?"

"Close, I'm thirty-five."

"I'm forty. So what do you do for a living?"

"I'm an attorney."

"That's good stuff. I'm a principal in a charter school."

"I love it. Our babies need to see more positive male role models. Good for you."

"Thank you, thank you. So what's your idea of a good time?"

"I love to eat."

"As tiny as you are? What do you eat? Bird food?"

"Ha! This little lady can put down some food and I make the best lasagna this side of the Ohio River."

"You'll have to cook dinner for me some time."

"Sure. I'd like that."

"What else should I know about you?"

"Hmmm. I go to church. I like to laugh. I love stimulating conversation. I don't have sex. I enjoy a drink on occasion. I—"

"Hold on. You don't have sex?"

"Nope. My goody box is out of service."

He rubbed his chin. "Well, Debra, your mower is all set. It shouldn't give you anymore trouble. Gotta go check on my folks. You have a good one."

"Oh, okay. I'll see you around."

"Uh huh."

Debra watched Douglas drive away. She replayed the conversation in her mind. Everything was going well until she mentioned that she was sexless. "So that dude was probably a hunter trying to use acts of service to get at my goody."

Debra finished the rest of the yard in a fraction of the time. She leaned against her car to admire her work and then called Doc Reed.

"Doc, I figured if I came out and told him that he wasn't getting any, he'd respect that. Instead, he ran. Should I not have told him about not giving up the goody box and just string him along?"

"Nah, you did right."

"He was a predator, wasn't he?"

"I think you ran off a would-be predator. When you told him that you weren't having sex, he figured it was going to be too much work for him."

"But who knows? If he came at me right, I may have

changed my mind."

"Not what I wanted to hear."

"Sorry, just keeping it real."

"Appreciate your honesty. Old boy figured he didn't have a chance."

"And he was not up for the challenge."

"Not at all. Now let me caution you. Some men will take a statement like that as a head-on challenge. They will step up their game in an effort to conquer the forbidden."

"See that's what I mean. Men are complicated." Exasperated, she blew air through her mouth until her lips vibrated.

"Not really. At the end of the day, it's still about getting to the goody box. You still have your box on lock?"

"Does the Rabbit 2000 count?" The call-waiting feature buzzed on her phone. "Hold on, Doc. Got a call coming in." She looked at the caller ID. "OMG! It's Jarrus!"

"Okay, then I'll talk at you later."

"No, hold on." She accepted the call. "Hey, Jarrus. How are you?"

"I'm good. And you?"

"I'm well. I'm on the other line. Can you hold on for a minute?"

"Sure."

She clicked over. "Doc?"

"Well, that was quick."

"He's holding on the other line. I need a pep talk."

"You can do it." He hung up the phone.

"Oh." She switched back to Jarrus. "Okay, I'm back."

"Did I catch you at a bad time?"

"No, no, you're good."

"So how've you been?"

"Pretty good. And you?"

"Been okay. How was Jamaica?"

"Absolutely wonderful. We had such a great time. I came back relaxed, rejuvenated, revived, re—"

"How about you *re*-connect with me this weekend? You've put me off long enough."

"It has been awhile, huh? Your timing couldn't be more perfect. My girlfriends and I are having a cookout this weekend."

"Me and three women?"

"No, silly. They'll be a couple of men there for you to compare sports teams and whatever else guys do."

"Cool. I just didn't want to be the only guy there and get caught up in a barrage of probing questions."

She giggled. "It's not that kind of event. Maybe next time."

"My focus is you and you only. Give me the details starting with what you're wearing."

"Saturday?"

"Right now."

Debra and Jarrus talked until the street lights came on. She ended the call, put the mower, gloves and car in the garage and then went in the house.

"I smell awful." She ran the bath water, added an extra capful of bubble bath and then slid into the tub. She rested her head on an inflatable tub pillow, closed her eyes for a few minutes. She washed, rinsed and repeated twice. Once in the soak cycle, she called Doc Reed.

"So how'd it go with Jarrus?"

"You definitely left me hanging."

"Do you have me on speakerphone? I hear an echo."

"Yep. You left me hanging."

"But you handled it, didn't you?"

"Actually, I did. We're getting together this weekend at Rachel's."

"I knew you had it in you."

"I'm getting there. Got a question for you?"

"Shoot."

"I get the whole in-pursuit-of-happiness thing, but why is it that when I'm not preoccupied with seeing him or giving up the goody, he seems pressed?"

Doc groaned.

"Catch you at a bad time? Sounds like you're into what you keep telling me to hibernate."

"'Pressed' did something to me deep inside."

"Why?

"When you say that a man is pressed, you're saying that he's out of control with emotion."

"He's a big girl, huh?"

"No, it goes deeper than that for a man. We don't like to think of ourselves as being weak or vulnerable even if it's true. We're supposed to be strong, in control and on top of our game at all times; at least that's what we tell ourselves. However, it's this same Goliath attitude that makes us such an easy target for David's slingshot. Meaning, our overly confident swagger can blind us to the fact that our heart has been stolen and we don't realize it until our woman pulls away. When it happens, we may try to act hard, but the reality is we can't eat, sleep or think until we get her back and that's the only way we feel in control again."

"Who would've thought?"

"Relationships are all about control and who has it. Not so much control as to manipulate, but rather who is setting the pace of the relationship. Typically, one person is running and the other is chasing."

"Cat and mouse games."

"It's just how the psychology of attraction works. So if he wanted your goody box and you didn't give it up, then you took the control: balance of power."

"Yeah, I like holding the reigns, being on top, riding bareback."

"I'm not sure I like where you're going with that." He cleared his throat. "Now he's going to be in hot pursuit of what he didn't get; your goodies. That doesn't necessarily mean that he's going to be all over you like an octopus every time you get together, but by holding out you've stimulated his chasing instinct just like the lion chasing the elusive gazelle. He'll be back, trust me."

"You love analogies, don't you?"

"Yes I do. They make the illustrations so much more vivid and thus easy to remember."

"Always a reason for your approach."

"Always. For the sake of argument, let's assume Jarrus is an ambusher-type hunter waiting for you to let your guard down so he can strike. The longer he pursues his prey without capturing it, the more likely he's becoming emotionally consumed with you. Before he realizes it, he's fallen in love and he's in too deep to pull out. He's concerned about you; not just your goody box."

"It just amazes me that all it takes is holding out."

"And because of your discipline, he transforms from an ambusher to a companion."

"And then it's time to get married." She wrung out the washcloth and let the water run down her chest.

"Whoa. Hold your horses, partner. The companion is a hunter too, but he hunts with a different motive. He's like a cowboy who spots the most beautiful, wild stallion he's ever seen. He says to himself, 'That's just the kind of horse I need.' He chases down the stallion and after he captures it, a deep genuine bond is formed between them."

"That time factor again."

"You got it. The companion hunter was not hunting to consume, but for a helper and a friend."

"Okay, so if he can stand the test of time, then he earns his rightful place as lifelong partner. Guess it's not really all that tough to comprehend after all."

"Not once the light bulb goes off in your mind."

"And goody box."

He chuckled. "And goody box. I'll let you in on a little secret. You're talking to an ex-ambusher turned companion."

"Yeah, you had mentioned that earlier, but it's hard to believe."

"It's true. I was the guy who befriended you, made you laugh, offered a shoulder to cry on and then strategically planned to attack my prey with military-like precision."

"You just don't seem like that kind of guy, Doc. I would have thought you were a companion always."

"I started out as a companion. One-woman man all day long, but after a couple of heart-wrenching relationships, I changed my strategy."

"Your guard went up."

"Yeah, women can be awful too, you know."

"I know it."

"We were in college when I met my wife, Ronelle. I had targeted her as just another victim."

"So what made her different?"

"She kept me in pursuit for so long that before I knew it, I was the victim."

"Not the relationship guru."

"I'm still a man."

"Understood."

"I compare how she snared me to cooking a frog. At first the water was nice, comfortable, at room temperature, so I felt in control. She turned up the heat a little at a time."

"Turned it up how? School me, Doc. A sistah needs to know all the tricks of the trade."

"It's not much to it, really. The more we spent time together the more comfortable I got with her. We went on formal dates, but it was the small, intimate things that had me in boiling water before I knew it."

"Oh, so you got to the goody box?"

"No, I'm talking about walks in the park, an ice-cream run, chilling on the couch watching a movie. We enjoyed each other's company all summer. That time with her became routine not as in monotonous, but expected; anticipated and when we fell out of the routine, I missed her. So while I'm thinking that I'm still in control and could pull out of the relationship at anytime, I was emotionally attached."

"Ha!"

"One day she told me that she wasn't just going to be one of my little friends once the fall semester started."

"Work it, Ronelle."

"And if I wasn't ready to fully commit, she could no longer continue to see me."

"Gotcha!"

"I thought I was going to jump out of the water, but to my surprise my legs didn't work. Even though the water was boiling, I was powerless to move."

"The froggy couldn't leap, huh?"

"At that point, I knew I wanted all of her, not just her goody box."

"Subtle, but effective."

"So now I'm like the guy who successfully swindled the Las Vegas casinos out of millions of dollars. Once I got caught, I made an agreement to help identify other hustlers to prevent them from doing what I did."

"That sounds like that movie with Leonardo DiCaprio; *Catch Me If You Can*. Well, I for one am glad that you're on our side. We're going to have to get you some bodyguards for revealing all these secrets."

"Already have a couple henchmen in mind."

"That's stupid."

"I'm serious."

"Oh. Hey, while I have you on the phone, got a few questions. Not so much for me, but for general knowledge."

"I can give you a few more minutes. It's almost time to tuck my girls in for the night."

"Well, give me the short answers. Why do men keep

women in the grey area with respect to exclusive dating?

"Commitment phobic."

"Why is it that almost every man expects sex?"

"Derived from the pattern of women allowing men to open their package without much effort."

"Why do some men believe that cheating is acceptable?"

"Men separate sex and love which makes it easy for them to cheat and not see the harm."

"How long is long enough before opening the goody-box gift?"

"You want the spiritual answer?"

"According to the Bible, it's until you're married, so what's the other answer?"

"Until he puts a ring on it as Beyoncé said. And that's not a friendship or engagement ring; that's a wedding ring."

Debra heard one of Doc Reed's daughters calling for him. "Did she just say, 'Daddy, look at me'?"

"Yep."

"How sweet. Okay, Doc. Let's pick this one up tomorrow."

~ ~ ~ ~ ~ ~ ~ ~

The next morning, as Debra power walked through her neighborhood, she called Doc Reed to continue the conversation.

"Debra, I'm having a hard time hearing you. What's that noise?"

"Oh, it's probably my hood rubbing on the Bluetooth. Can't let this morning dew mess up my 'do." She disconnected the Bluetooth and put the cell phone to her ear. "Is that better?"

"Much."

"Okay, give me more insight into this balance-of-power thing."

"Few experience relationships where both people have mutual levels of love and respect. The more relationship-savvy person may use devices to manipulate the flow instead of doing what's right for the relationship."

"Now that's game playing."

"Right. Whoever loves the least controls the relationship."

"And he who discloses first, loses."

"Very good, Grasshopper."

"Thank you, sensei."

"Got another illustration for you."

"I'd be disappointed if you didn't."

"This one depicts a man's commitment level."

"That's what I want to know."

"You have tire kickers and buyers. A tire kicker walks into the showroom, suited up, giving the appearance that he's serious about making a purchase. He asks the right questions to learn about the features of the car, gives up his driver's license to test drive the car and even lets the dealer run his credit knowing all along that his credit score is 400 and he cannot afford the payments."

"Sounds kind of parasitic, too."

"Oh, he is definitely a hunter. In contrast, the buyer is committed to the process before he even walks into the dealership. He does the same things as the tire kicker, but he is prepared to close the deal. His credit is right; he has the down payment; he knows the terms that work best for him and leaves the dealership in his new ride."

"Now that's the companion. He knew what he wanted and went for it."

"Your hunter-detecting skills are improving."

"I know it."

"Here's another scenario: you're looking to buy a used car."

"Uh, Doc, you just gave me the tire-kicker-versus-buyer scenario. Do I need to call 9-1-1 for you?"

"Debra, this is not regurgitated praise. Got something new for you."

"Oh, my bad."

"As I was saying, you're looking for a used car and you

find one that calls out your name. You have to have it, so you negotiate with the used-car salesman on the terms."

"Sounds like the same illustration."

"Now this dude sees how committed you are to buying that particular car, so to seal the deal, he tells you that he has another buyer."

"Lying to make me move to action."

"Right. It's the sense of loss that makes you move hastily without thinking through all of your options."

"Those dang-blasted emotions. Do we ever grow out of them?"

"Sorry to say, but no. You can be seventy years old and still get schoolgirl stupid when a toothless geriatric walks by."

"Bummer. Had hoped to get past all this at some point."

"Back to the used car. A little more searching and you would've noticed that the brakes didn't work, the head gasket was damaged and it leaked oil."

"So you buy the jacked-up car and you're left with costly repairs and unreliable transportation."

"Aw, I can't get anybody to say amen to that right there."

"I can honestly say that I've been that naïve used-car buyer pressured into making a deal that was more hassle than it was worth. But I'm a reformed believer now. Hallelu-shah!"

"And the moral of the story…."

"Don't go by what a man says, but rather watch what he does. His actions are the true litmus test to his motives."

Chapter 24

Something's Changed

Rachel fantasized about Conrad as she prepared the typical Friday-night dinner for her family: spaghetti with marinara sauce and garlic bread. She wondered what he was doing and if he was "doing" anyone this weekend. She looked forward to Mondays. Back to work, back to Conrad. Other than a couple of extended lunch excursions—with coordinated arrivals and departures to shun the appearance of being together—they were cautious not to bring unwanted attention to their business-friendly interactions.

She smiled at the thought of Conrad salvaging her company, bringing focus to her chaotic life, filling her empty tank.

The scorched ground turkey caused the smoke detector to alert. Brian jumped up from the family-room couch, ran into the kitchen.

"You okay?"

"I wasn't paying attention and fooled around and burnt the meat." She scraped the singed poultry into the garbage disposal, cleaned the skillet.

He fanned an unopened piece of junk mail at the detector. "What's going on with you lately?"

"What do you mean?"

"You seem preoccupied."

She grabbed another pound of ground turkey, peeled back the packaging, dropped it in the skillet. "Got a lot on my mind."

"The business?"

"Among other things."

"How about I take you out to lunch on Monday? We haven't done a nooner in awhile."

Rachel turned up her lip. "Nah, that's okay. I don't have time to play on the job. No sense making the trip and then I can't get away."

"I don't mind. If you're not available, I'll chat with Sylvia or better yet, chop it up with that new guy. What's his name?"

The hairs on Rachel's neck stood at attention. Her heart pulsed faster as she thought about Brian and Conrad 'chopping it up' about her. She used the oven mitt to dab at the droplets of sweat on her forehead. "Conrad."

"Yeah, Conrad. I'd like to thank the man who's been helping you keep RJ Nance afloat."

"Uh, I'd rather you didn't, honey."

"Why? You never minded me stopping by in the past."

"Well, things are a lot different since the Bob fiasco. It's tough enough keeping the team focused on maintaining current clients and finding new ones, without having to entertain the boss' husband."

"Entertain?"

"Yeah, they get a little antsy when you're around. Guess they see you as an informant of sorts." She gave a half-grin, hoping that Brian bought the line.

"I can see that." He nodded. "I don't want to stir up the office, so how about we plan to do something this weekend?"

"Sherry's party is tomorrow."

"That's right. I forgot."

"So is that your way of saying that you didn't look for the

badminton set yet?"

"Actually I found it, but it's not useable. The last time we played, I tripped over Mogli. I bent the pole and ripped the net."

She chuckled. "That was hilarious." She looked at Brian who was not entertained by her laughter. "I'm sorry, babe, but it was. You fell in slow motion." She re-enacted the fall grabbing at the air, eyes wide, mouth open.

"Not funny. I could've been hurt."

She wiped the tears from her eyes, snorted. "The only thing that was hurt was your ego. Admit it; it was funny."

He displayed a smiling frown. "I have to get a new set."

"Okay." She cupped her hands over her mouth. "I want it up and ready before the guests arrive."

"And what time is that?"

"I've taken care of the menu, the caterer, activities and...." She looked at him, shook her head. "Just have it in place by noon. Can you do that for me?"

"I got it."

Chapter 25

Wait for Love

Jarrus struck home plate with another wonderful date. He put some time into planning the smallest details. He said and did all the right things to make Debra feel special. The old Debra would have been in the prone position getting her middle tickled. The new Debra oscillated between the thought of gratification today or commitment tomorrow.

Jarrus walked her to the front door. "Can I come in for coffee?"

She looked into his eyes, envisioned him taking her to ecstasy. "You can stay long enough for one," she held her finger in the air for emphasis, "one cup of coffee."

He smiled, followed her into the family room.

"Have a seat. I'll start the coffee." She slipped off her shoes and departed for the kitchen.

Jarrus sat on the couch, admired the splendor of Debra's home. "I love your art. I have that one." He pointed to a double-matted framed picture of one Black man reaching down to pull up another. "*He Ain't Heavy* by Gilbert Young."

"I love it. Do you take cream and sugar?"

"Yes, thanks."

Debra returned carrying a tray.

Jarrus stood. "Here, let me take that."

"Thanks."

He set the tray on the coffee table.

Debra poured coffee into two non-matching mugs. "How many teaspoons of sugar?"

"Two."

"And cream?"

"Until it's the shade of you."

She blushed, smiled, prepared his coffee. *He can hold his breath for about three months before revealing his true motives.* "Here you go." She sat.

"Thanks." He sipped. "Perfect." He set the mug on the table, rested his arm on the back of the couch, behind Debra.

"My coffee needs more cream." She scooted to the edge of the couch, added cream, stirred, tasted, repeated several times.

"I'm not going to hurt you. You know that, right?"

That's what you say. "Of course I do."

"Then slide yourself back here and sit next to me."

Debra took a few more sips. She reclined with coffee in hand as a small but effective barrier. She crossed her legs at the ankles; another barrier. "How's your coffee?"

He chuckled. "Perfect, remember?"

"Oh yeah." Her feet twitched.

"Why are you nervous?"

"I'm not nervous."

"Then why are your feet jumping a mile a minute?"

She stopped fidgeting. "Guess I am a little nervous."

"Why?"

Instead of replying, she recalled Doc Reed's advice. *He who discloses first, loses.* She wanted to tell Jarrus that her goody box was ripe for the picking and that she really liked him. But what would he do with that information? Toy with her heart? Pursue the goody box? Ravage her and then leave her carcass for the vultures?

As she strategized her next move, Jarrus moved in to kiss

her. She inhaled, closed her eyes, parted her lips, waited.

"Where are you going?"

"Huh?" She opened her eyes, exhaled. Debra had leaned away from him and held the coffee mug at breast level.

Jarrus took the mug, set it on the table, pulled Debra close. He put his arm around her to keep her from drifting away again. Hog tied. He whispered, "I promise I won't do anything you don't want me to do," and then nibbled on her ear.

Debra's heart beat faster, her nipples stood at attention, her goody box cheered. "Oh, Jarrus." She squirmed to thwart the pulsating spasms.

He kissed her cheek and then her lips.

She responded. As their passion ensued, Doc Reed's words reverberated in her mind. *Men separate love and sex.* She wondered if Jarrus was an ambusher or companion. *Only time will tell.*

"Jarrus?"

"Yeah, baby." He went back to nibbling on her ear.

"You have no idea how much I want to do this...."

"Me, too."

"But...."

"Your butt is beautiful." He lavished her with a series of pecks as she tried to speak.

"But I can't."

"Yes you can. I'll be gentle." He caressed her stimulated bosom.

"Jarrus!" She pushed him away. "I cannot go there again."

The advance stopped. He rubbed his chin, looked at her for a moment. "I can respect that." He nodded, stood. "Thanks for the coffee."

"I'm sorry." She began to stand.

He put up his hand. "No, don't apologize and don't get up. I'll see myself out."

She plopped onto the couch as he walked out the front

door. She wanted to call 911 to report a robbery in progress—Jarrus had taken her heart—but instead she called Doc Reed.

"Hey, Doc. This is Debra."

"Hey, Debra. Are you okay?" Doc Reed panted.

"Not really. Why are you out of breath? Are you having sex?"

"What? No, I'm on the elliptical machine." He chuckled. "I do not accept calls when I'm entering into the holy of holies."

"That's so stupid."

"So what's going on? Things didn't go well with Jarrus?"

"The date was great, but…."

"Reverend, did you come short of the glory?"

"Reverend? Don't speak that on me."

"It's just a term I use. Nothing prophetic."

"Oh, okay."

"So did you give up the goody goody goody box?"

She blurted out a groan from deep within. "No!"

"Well, that's a good thing."

"It doesn't feel good." She whined. "I had to fight to keep him at bay."

"He forced himself on you?"

"No, I had to fight me. I wanted to jump him, but *you* kept popping in my head." She mimicked. "Don't trust what he says because men will say anything to get to the goody box. You're a wounded doe." She yelped.

"Does it help to know that I am proud of you? I know it wasn't easy for you, but you did it. And the next time—"

"The next time? He's not coming back."

"The next time will be easier."

"Jarrus is gone forever."

"If not Jarrus, then John, Jack or Joseph. But there will be another man."

"How can you be so sure when I'm not?"

"There aren't any guarantees in this relationship thing, but knowing men like I do, another will come."

"I guess."

"But if you're desperate, he's gone after he's done."

"The adventures of the goody box."

"Since you won't take my word for it, talk to Sherry. She's been where you are now and can better relate to what you're feeling."

"Now that's sound advice. I'll talk at you later."

The call had barely disconnected when Debra punched in Sherry's digits.

"Hey, Sherry."

"Hey, Ms. Deb, how'd it go with Jarrus?"

"Great, until I put him out."

"You put him out?"

"It was the only way I could keep from having sex."

Sherry cheered. "Woo hoo! You go, girl!"

"It's not a celebration."

"Of course it is. You took control of you. Don't you feel liberated and empowered?"

"Maybe a little, mixed in with lots of sexual frustration and fear."

"You're afraid that he won't come back, but that's not on you, that's on him. You did what was best for Debra. If Jarrus can accept that, great. If not, then why would you want to invest anymore time into someone whose objective is to hit it and quit it? You deserve more than that and now you're believing it."

"You think?"

"I know. What you did won't be detrimental to Jarrus."

"Except that he left rock hard."

"It wasn't the first time and won't be the last. But if you had yielded to the penis, the result would have been detrimental to you. You would have digressed to your old ways and gotten...." She waved her hand like a *Price Is Right* model.

"The same old results."

"Exactly. Wondering what he's doing; if he's going to call."

"I do that now."

"Yeah, but not on the wham-bam-thank-you-ma'am side of things. You are in a better place. It may not feel like it, but you are. Trust me."

"And if he never calls?"

"You'll be okay."

"That's easy for you to say. You have Dwight."

"No, it's because I am where I am with Dwight that I can say that. It hasn't been easy for me, but I made a conscious decision to love me first. And because I am into me, he's into me, too. It's weird, I know, but it is what it is. I made the declaration to put my box on lock as a member of The Goody Box Club."

"The what?"

"The Goody Box Club. It's a support network of women who have been empowered to protect the goody box. Our slogan is 'My box is on lock!' We chat online, check on each other's progress and there's talk of an annual conference at a resort—a full weekend of pampering, encouragement and enlightenment."

"Why can't relationships be easier? E-Harmony seems to have it down to a science."

"I bet you better not."

"I thought about it. A girl from church did it and landed herself a world-renowned operatic tenor. She travels from continent to continent with him. They are loving each other and enjoying life."

"Okay, and what about the bazillion other folks who pay the fee, fill out the profile and never find a partner? I have more horror stories of online dating than you have of successes, so let's not go tit-for-tat on this one. At the end of the day, the true test is do you trust God?"

"I trust Him, but not completely."

"That's like being a little pregnant or a little dead. Either you trust Him or you don't. Which one is it?"

"I will trust Him."

"Like Donnie McClurkin sings, 'Who else can I turn to?'" Sherry lifted her hand in reverence. "That song takes me in every time. Let me hear you say it again, but with more confidence."

"I will trust Him!"

"Trust Him with what?"

"Me!"

Chapter 26

The Cookout

The caterer arrived at Rachel's house as scheduled. The weatherman indicated that the unseasonably warm temperatures would reach the mid-80s, so instead of eating on the deck, she opted for the enclosed patio. It had all of the conveniences of being outside—sunlight, fresh air, view of the yard—without the hassle of bugs and sweat. She turned the three ceiling fans on high and then explained to the caterer how she wanted the food displayed.

As she confirmed that her expectations were understood, she noticed that the badminton net was not in place. She walked into the house.

"Brian, you promised you'd take care of the badminton."

"Oh, babe. I forgot."

"But we just talk—"

"I said 'I forgot.' I'll take care of it now." He grabbed the keys, headed for the door.

"Take the kids with you. I can't keep an eye on them and get ready."

"I'll take your SUV then."

"That's fine." She ran upstairs, changed clothes and then went back to the patio to supervise.

The doorbell chimed.

Rachel opened the door. "Hey, Debra."

"Hey, sweetie." They kissed cheeks. "Here you go." She handed Rachel a sweet potato cheesecake.

"Oh my goodness. You know how I love your dessert. Thanks for bringing it, but you didn't have to bring anything."

"I know, but I wanted to show Jarrus how well I can cook."

Rachel looked around Debra, stepped out onto the porch. She put her hand to her forehead and then moved as if searching for a far-off stranger. "You're having delusions of grandeur too, huh?"

"Very funny. He's coming after he gets off work." She walked past Rachel. Mogli wagged his tail, jumped on her. "Hey, Stinker Doodle." Debra rubbed him. "Fresh haircut, huh?"

"He was long overdue."

"Shampoochies puts the cutest bandanas on him. What's on this one?" She squatted to get a closer look. "Are those bones?"

"Uh, yeah. Do you need glasses?"

"I'm just saying. Mogli doesn't have any teeth so he definitely can't enjoy a bone."

"You better leave my baby alone. He can eat just fine." She changed her tone to a mother talking ga-ga-goo-goo with her newborn. "Ain't that right, Meme's baby?"

Mogli trotted over to her, ran in circles.

"What in the world is wrong with your dog?"

"He's excited. He loves his mommy."

"Okay, ixnay the baby talk. The food smells great." She walked toward the kitchen.

Rachel placed the cheesecake in the refrigerator. "Only the best for my girls. Come on, let's sit on the patio."

Debra followed Rachel out the door off the kitchen. Mogli trotted behind them. They sat on the wicker couch.

"He's still running in circles. You excite him like that?"

"I do, but that's his Mommy-I-have-to-go-potty dance. You can't tell the difference?" She stood, opened the door to the yard, talked over her shoulder. "Don't feel bad. No one else in the house can read him either. Only him mommy."

Mogli darted from one end of the backyard to the other with his tongue and bandana flapping freely.

"Ooooooooooookay."

"I'm not crazy."

"No, you're just a dog whisperer."

The caterer said, "Excuse me, Ms. Nance. We're finished. Do you have anything else you'd like us to take care of before we leave?"

"No thank you." She stood to inspect the meal. "The display looks wonderful. Do you mind going out this door?" She pointed to the patio door.

"Not at all."

"Watch out for my dog."

"Yes, ma'am. Thank you for your business. Have a great party."

"Will do." She watched the van back out of the driveway and then turned to Debra. "I finally get to meet Jarrus and Dwight."

"I know, right?"

"So holding out worked for you, too."

"Yep. I didn't think I'd ever hear from Jarrus again, but he called the next day."

"Good for you."

"Where are the kids?"

"With Brian. As usual he didn't come through, so he's running around trying to make it right."

"Ease off the guy. At least he's trying."

"Trying to what? Drive me to the brink of insanity and then kick me over the edge?"

"Geezo, it's like that?"

"It is for me. You could blindfold me, spin me around twenty times and then let me go. How I'd walk is how I feel.

Disoriented."

The kids came running through the backyard screaming and crying. Rachel and Debra jumped off the couch and ran to meet them.

Rachel said, "What's wrong? Why are you guys hollering like that?"

Between sobs, BJ said, "It was an accident."

"What was an accident?" Rachel ran toward the side of the house.

Marcus said, "He didn't mean to do it!"

"Where's Charisse?"

"In the Honda."

Just as Rachel rounded the corner she saw Brian kneeling on the driveway.

"Brian, what happened?" She ran to him.

With his head bowed, he said, "I am so sorry."

She looked over his shoulder and saw Mogli, bleeding from every orifice. Rachel grabbed her stomach, hyperventilated. "What did you do?" She pushed Brian, dropped to her knees. "Mogli!" she cried.

Debra grabbed Charisse out of the car seat. "Come on, boys." She took them in the house.

"I was pulling into the garage. I didn't see him."

"He's still breathing. Get a blanket. We're going to the vet."

"I'm so—"

"Get a blanket!"

Brian grabbed a blanket from the trunk of his car, handed it to Rachel.

Tears cascaded down her cheeks as she wrapped the blanket around Mogli. He whimpered when she picked him up. "It's okay, baby. Mommy's got you."

Brian helped her in the car and then sped off for the emergency animal clinic on Dryden Road.

Rachel rocked Mogli, gently rubbed his head and cried. *Not him too, Lord.*

By the time they arrived at the clinic, Mogli had died. Rachel bellowed for an hour before mustering the strength to take him inside.

Brian opened the car door, reached for Mogli.

"Don't you touch him!"

When they entered the clinic, Brian talked with the receptionist.

Rachel sat in the waiting area and watched a family play with their dog with a cast on its hind leg. She pet Mogli and tears pooled onto the blood-soaked blanket.

The receptionist approached her.

"Would you like me to take him for you?"

Rachel looked up at her, shook her head.

"Then let me get you a room." She walked away and returned a few minutes later. "Follow me, Mrs. Monroe."

Brian helped Rachel stand and supported her as she walked into the room, dazed and distraught. She sat in the chair and rocked Mogli. Brian leaned against the wall, quiet.

Thirty minutes later, Rachel stood.

Brian moved to help her. "What can I do, babe?"

"Nothing." She laid Mogli on the steel table. Unwrapped him, cried. "I don't want to let him go."

"We can stay as long as you need." He rubbed her back.

She jerked away.

Brian's cell phone rang. He looked at the caller ID, handed the phone to Rachel. "It's Debra."

Her head was heavy, so she let it droop. "Hello."

"Hey, Rachel. How's Mogli?"

She sniffed. "He's gone."

"I'm so sorry. I know how much he meant to you."

Silent; tears fell.

"I fed the kids, put the food in the fridge and locked up the house. The kids are at your mother's."

Rachel mumbled incoherent babble and then said, "Thanks."

"Can I do anything to help you?"

"No. Thank you for taking care of the kids and the house." She began to cry. "I have to go now." She let the phone drop, laid over Mogli and cried. About an hour later, with her tears depleted, Rachel left Mogli at the clinic.

When the Monroes returned home, Rachel went upstairs. She climbed into bed without taking off her clothes. Lying in the fetal position, she reached on the side of the bed to rub Mogli. When her hand didn't find his soft mane, she cried herself to sleep.

The next morning, when she got up to use the bathroom, she looked out the window. Brian was washing the blood out of the driveway. As the red water pooled at the curb, Rachel withdrew.

~ ~ ~ ~ ~ ~ ~ ~

Unable to maintain any semblance of emotional stability, Rachel called Conrad.

"Hey, Ms. Nance. To what do I owe this Sunday call?"

In a weak voice, she said, "Hey, Conrad."

"What's wrong?"

"I won't be in for a couple of days. Can you cover for me?"

"Sure. But tell me what's wrong? Are you sick? Do you need me to do anything for you?"

Rachel sobbed. "My dog died yesterday."

Conrad released a moan of empathy. "I am sorry to hear that."

"Thanks."

"I have the office under control, so don't worry about that. You take care of yourself."

"Thanks."

"Rach?"

"Yes?"

"If you need me, you know I'm here for you, right?"

"Yes, I do. Thanks."

~ ~ ~ ~ ~ ~ ~ ~

After a couple of days of grieving, Rachel returned to

work. As expected, Sylvia was at her post.

"Ms. Nance, I'm very sorry about your dog."

"Thanks, Sylvia. Hold my calls, please."

"Yes, ma'am."

Rachel slouched in her chair, stared at the family picture, cried. When she opened the lap drawer of the desk, she saw an envelope with her name printed on it. She opened the envelope, read the note.

> *Rach,*
>
> *I'm sorry about Mogli. I know how much he meant to you. I wanted to call or stop by, but didn't want to intrude. So this note is my way of letting you know that I thought about you often.*
>
> *Conrad*
>
> *P.S. I hope you don't mind, but I informed Shampoochies, the vet and the Humane Society about Mogli. They have been instructed to remove you from their mailing lists. I didn't want you to get a reminder notice months from now and then relive this awful situation all over again.*

A slight smile washed on her face. She had lost yet another significant male, but had acquired a new one. Conrad had proven himself to be reliable, dependable and trustworthy. When she was at her lowest, he was there to help her; showering her with kind words and acts of service that made her life a little less hectic.

She tapped the intercom. "Sylvia, when's my next business trip?"

"You have a meeting in San Diego in two weeks."

"Have the arrangements been finalized?"

"Yes, ma'am. Conrad took care of that yesterday. You leave on Wednesday the fifth and return Friday at six in the evening."

"Very good. Thanks."

She received a text message on her cell phone.

Conrad: Are you okay?

Rachel: Yes, thanks. Didn't see you this morning. You in?

Conrad: Yes. Didn't want to come to your office.

Rachel: Why?

Conrad: Because I want to hug you past your pain.

Rachel: Aw, how sweet.

Conrad: Inappropriate. Sorry for disrespecting you.

Rachel: No disrespect. I appreciate the concern. Thanks for taking care of Mogli and my flight arrangements.

Conrad: No problem. I'm here for you.

Rachel: Thanks.

Conrad: Can I be honest with you?

Rachel: Of course.

Conrad: I thought about booking a flight for me too.

Chapter 27

Can't Put a Price on Peace of Mind

A few days before her business trip, Rachel coordinated the demands of her personal life with Sherry. They met at Panera Bread on Brown Street.

"I'm leaving for San Diego on Wednesday."

"That sounds wonderful. Want me to join you?"

"Nah. After I'm done sucking up to the client," she giggled, "I need some time alone. Besides, I need you and Debra to help Brian with the kids. He can't seem to get himself together, since ''

"I'm sure he feels awful."

"I guess. If only he'd done like I asked, when I asked, maybe Mogli would still be alive."

"Don't do that to yourself or Brian. It was an accident."

"That's what he keeps saying, but I'm not sure."

Sherry jerked her neck, glared at Rachel. "What in the world?"

"I know, I'm trippin'. He loved Mogli." She paused.

"Another Mogli moment?"

"Yeah, but I'm getting better."

"I hate that you missed Dwight. He was looking forward

to finally meeting you."

"We'll have to plan another outing. I didn't have my camera to capture the Casper sighting anyway."

"Casper the friendly ghost?"

"You know it or Sasquatch, the abominable snowman, Loch Ness Monster, aliens…."

"Aliens are real. I don't care what you say, I don't believe that God made all those stars and planets and the only one with life is this one. Adam and Eve jacked us all up, so someone, somewhere had to get it right."

"So Dwight is as real as the aliens?"

"Don't go there, Rachel. Please, don't go there."

"Did Debra see this imaginary playmate of yours?"

"Actually, no. By the time we arrived, she had already left with the kids."

"Uh huh."

Sherry bowed her head. With upturned eyes, she said, "Promise you won't get mad at me."

"Oh, Lord. What now?"

"Just promise."

Rachel put her hands under the table, crossed her fingers. "I promise."

"You and Debra have seen Dwight; you just didn't know who he was."

"No, we missed him at the airport."

"Not talking about the airport."

"Then out with it, woman. When did we see Dwight?"

"Remember the night we were at Therapy Café?"

Rachel gasped. "If you tell me that Sexual Chocolate is your Dwight, I'm going to fall out." She erupted into laughter. "Yep, he's Sasquatch all right."

"No, Rachel. My guy was at the bar. You noticed him looking at me."

She pondered, tapped her index finger on her forehead. "Aw man, I remember commenting that he was a handsome brother, but I definitely cannot recall what he looked like."

"Well, don't blame me for your failing memory."

"That's so not right. Wait 'til I tell Debra. She'll be able to recall what he looks like."

"Doubt it. She was tossing aimlessly in her perfect storm of Vincent and Jarrus."

"No wonder you came in there all dolled up. You guys playing meet-the-stranger-at-the-bar for thrills?"

"A lady doesn't kiss and tell."

"Lady, how can you have anything to tell if you don't kiss?"

"You are demented."

"Now that you've found some poor man to project your Dwightism complex onto, let's get back to the matter at hand." She looked at Sherry from the corners of her eyes, shook her head. "I'm going to e-mail you and Debra the kids' activities for the week. Can you check on Brian to make sure that he follows through?"

"Sure, no problem. Is Conrad assisting you while you're out of the office?"

Rachel tensed, fell back in her seat. "Huh? Why would you ask me that?"

"Because he's your office manager and that's what he does."

She smacked herself on the forehead, gave a nervous giggle. "I am so distracted today. Of course he's assisting. He's running the office in my absence."

"Alrighty then. I need you to focus. You have to go before that client sharp and on point."

"True, true, true."

"How's it going with you and Brian?"

"About the same. Co-existing under the same roof."

"Roommates."

"Yeah, something like that."

"My girlfriend Rhonda gave me a great illustration." She grabbed a piece of paper and pen.

"You and your illustrations."

"Love is a continuum from zero to one hundred percent." She drew a horizontal line, added the numbers at the end points. "A man buys you flowers; you give him ten percent of your love." She leap-frogged the pen from zero to ten. "He takes you out on a great date, you give him twenty percent." She hopped the pen to the thirty. "He loves you, protects you, marries you." She bounced the pen several times to the end of the line. "You have given him all the love that you have to offer. You are fully committed to this man and would give your life for him."

"Okay, your point is…." She held out her hands, palms up.

"Hold on. Now let's say that he forgot your birthday, he loses some points." She drew a half circle from one hundred back to ninety. "Then he—"

"He kills your dog."

Sherry sneered at Rachel. "It was an accident."

She tightened her lips. "Minus forty."

"I'll give you twenty and that's it."

"How about thirty?"

"Twenty is my final offer."

"I'll take it."

Sherry drew a line back to seventy. "And God forbid he should cheat on you." She bounced the pen back to twenty. "Now he will bust his tail to make it right. Do all the things he knows make you happy and he may gain back some of your love." She skipped the pen forward a few spaces. "But he'll never get back to one hundred. When a man hurts a woman, it's tough for him to get back her fully committed love because she doesn't trust him enough to let him back in."

"Like R. Kelly said, 'When a woman's fed up, ain't nothing you can do about it.'"

"When your mind has made up its mind, it's over."

"Shuna-ma."

"I-bought-a-Kia-should-a-bought-a-Honda."

They laughed.

Sherry looked Rachel in the eyes. "All jokes aside, you have to figure out how to release Brian or you're going to regret it."

Rachel harrumphed. "E tu, Brute?"

"Rachel, I'm not turning against you. I'm trying to help you."

"Save my marriage?"

"Your peace of mind."

Chapter 28

Batman and Rachel

A few days before departing on business trips, Rachel uses a checklist to ensure that she packs the essentials—presentation material, laptop, passport when applicable. As part of the packing ritual, she tosses outfits from the dedicated-for-travel section of her closet into the suitcase, careful to coordinate accessories. She packs three extra outfits just in case the client invites her to the skybox at a sporting event, a dinner gala or house party. Over the course of her career, she had amassed an abundance of frequent-flyer miles and mastered the art of traveling light: one carry-on and her super-sized purse which doubled as a laptop bag.

The advanced preparation minimized her travel anxiety, but not the stress. In addition to prepping for the client meeting and getting the kids together, she had duty booty with Brian. She enlisted for the assignment a couple years ago when he accused her of going AWOL—absent without lovemaking.

About midnight, spent from the rush of the day, she accommodated her husband and then tried to rest. But with the cares of life bouncing around in her head throughout the night, she ended up sleepless in Dayton.

Wednessday morning, as Rachel lay with her back to Brian, he went for round two.

"Rach, you awake?"

She feigned deep sleep.

"Rach?" He gently pushed on her shoulder. "Babe, are you asleep?"

She shooed him with her elbow.

"Come on, babe. I know you're not asleep."

She gave an extended sigh. "What do you want?"

"You know what I want."

"You cannot be serious." She slapped the bed. "I just gave you some last night."

"I know, but I didn't satisfy you."

"I'm good."

"Okay, then I didn't satisfy me."

She rolled over, flopped like a floundering fish out of water, slapped her arms across her chest. "Hurry up, Brian. I have a flight to catch."

"You sure?"

"It's now or never."

As Brian worked to purge the urge, Rachel rehearsed the travel itinerary in her mind. *I put the kids' schedules on the board and Sylvia made a copy for Brian to keep in the car. Did I put it in his car? Yeah, I did. Remind BJ to get his inhaler when he stays the night with Timmy on Thursday.*

He grunted.

"My flight returns on Friday, but you know how these trips go, so if I have a change in plans, I'll let you know."

"Yeah, yeah. I'm trying to concentrate."

Rachel looked over at the clock. She had just enough time to dress, see the kids off to school and dart to the airport. For some reason, Brian was going for the long-distance relay race and had already surpassed his usual three-minute dash.

She rubbed his hair, moaned and flexed. Brian reached the finish line and then Rachel sprinted to the bathroom.

~ ~ ~ ~ ~ ~ ~

Towing the carry-on with one hand and gripping the strap of her purse with the other, Rachel cleared through the security checkpoint and then zipped to the terminal. Her cell phone rang.

"Good morning, Rachel Nance."

"Hey, Rach. You get off okay?"

"Hey, Conrad. I'm headed toward the gate now. Got a slow start this morning."

"You're still making good time. You'll have a couple of minutes to catch your breath before boarding."

"Everything cool so far in the office?"

In a smug manner, he said, "Of course."

She giggled. "Silly of me to think otherwise."

"Yes indeed."

"Good morning. Thank you."

"You talking to me?"

"No, a man in the airport just greeted me and handed me a fresh tulip."

"Wow. That's nice. You don't see that often."

"I know it." She paused. "What in the world?"

"What's wrong?"

"Let me call you back." Rachel ended the call, stood in amazement. In the corridor leading to her departure gate, was a line of men, each holding a different type of fresh-cut flower. As Rachel passed a gentleman, he bowed, handed her a flower and wished her a safe and productive trip. By the time she got to the gate, she had a dozen flowers. Her cell phone rang.

Conrad said, "You okay?"

"I'm speechless. I'm not sure what just happened."

"Well, since I couldn't go with you, I wanted to send you off right."

"You did this?" Rachel's happiness beamed through the fiber optic network.

"Yeah, you know how I do."

"But how?"

"Come on now, I'm resourceful like that. I reached into my utility belt and worked my magic."

"You're not Bateman, you're Batman."

They laughed.

The ticket agent announced that the flight to San Diego was boarding.

"You're in first class this time."

"How'd you work that? Upgraded me using my reward miles?"

"No, just know that I'm well-connected." He paused. "Have a safe trip, Rach."

"Thanks, Batman."

"Call me when you land so I know that you made it in okay."

"Most definitely." Rachel boarded the airplane.

The male flight attendant assigned to first class assisted her with the carry-on and put it in the overhead storage compartment.

"Thank you."

"You are welcome, Ms. Nance." He handed her a box of Godiva gourmet chocolates.

"Oh, I love first class."

"These are compliments of Mr. Conrad Bateman."

She smiled.

As the pilot announced the weather, estimated arrival time and that the non-smoking light was on, Rachel received a text.

Conrad: I miss you already.
Rachel: Thanks for the chocolates. They're my favorite.
Conrad: I know. See you Friday.
Rachel: Not coming into office after trip.
Conrad: See you Friday.
Rachel: Huh?
Conrad: Planned post-trip unwind time.
Rachel: Why?
Conrad: You will need to be replenished.
Rachel: You're probably right.
Conrad: And I'm the man to see that it happens.
Rachel: How will I be replenished?
Conrad: Let me take care of that. You just enjoy it.
Rachel: I'm intrigued.
Conrad: I know.
Rachel: Gotta go. Cell phones off.
Conrad: Will send details Friday. Safe travels.
Rachel: K

~ ~ ~ ~ ~ ~ ~

With the three-hour time difference, Rachel arrived in southern California in time to catch a cab to the client's office. En route, she called Conrad and Brian—in that order—to confirm her safe arrival. She wowed the clients during the four-hour meeting and then checked in at the hotel. She caught a thirty-minute catnap, before dressing for the evening soiree. Thursday was just as hectic, but ended a few hours earlier at ten p.m. Pacific Time.

When she retired to the hotel, she confirmed the seven a.m. wake-up call. Rachel intertwined her fingers, put her clasped hands behind her head, reclined on the bed, closed her eyes. She let her thoughts carry her to a serene location. No clients, no kids, no worries. She lingered in that tranquil place, free of distractions and expectations. The only sound was a soft ambient whisper of rolling tides on a sandy beach. The waves lulled her to sleep.

~ ~ ~ ~ ~ ~ ~

Sitting in the hotel lobby, waiting for the cab, Rachel called Conrad.

"Hey, Batman. How's it going?"

"That's funny. I'm good, Rach. I heard that you showed out at the meeting."

"How did you…. Never mind, I don't want to know. Resourceful."

"Exactly. Are you ready for the details of your replenishment?"

"Yes." She nibbled on the complimentary pastry provided by the hotel.

"I have a spa day planned for you."

"Oh, that does sound nice."

"I tried to schedule it for Friday, but they were booked."

"So what are you saying?"

"Your pampering is Saturday."

"Hmm."

"What?"

"Once I'm home, I won't be able to get away."

"I figured as much, so I reserved a room for you at Crowne Plaza."

"Oh my."

"What?"

"Feels deceitful."

"Why? You deserve some time to yourself."

"I do, don't I?"

"Don't bother with checking in. Just go to Room 319. Dinner will be waiting for you."

Uncertain about the potential chain of events, Rachel sought clarification. "And where will you be waiting?"

"Where do you want me to wait?"

"What does that mean?"

"Rach, let's not toy with each other. You know that I have feelings for you and I believe the feelings are mutual."

"Yes, but—"

"I'm not asking you to do anything you don't want to do. Let's just spend some time together and see what happens."

"As friends, right? Nothing more."

"If that's your way of asking about sex, I'll leave that up to you."

"I set the pace?"

"You set the pace."

"I mean, I am mad at Brian and he's hurt me in so many ways, but I am still his wife."

"And I respect that. We're just friends trying to help each other through a rough patch."

"Okay, when do I need to let you know?"

"Everything's in place. If you choose to eat dinner and then leave, I'll see you Monday at work. No harm. No foul."

"And if I choose to stay?"

"I'll see you tonight."

Rachel pondered Conrad's proposition. She smacked her hand for toying with the idea and then discounted it as whimsical folly. She called Brian.

"Hey, babe. How are the kids?"

"They're good. Everything went well."

"Good. Did Debra and Sherry call?"

"Yep. Debra took Charisse to her dance class yesterday. She likes that stuff."

"Wonderful."

"So where are you now?"

"Still at the hotel. Look, uh...." She paused, unable to manage a forthright lie.

"You there?"

"Yeah, bad reception. I'm going to stay until Saturday. Just like I figured, the client wants to introduce me to some other folks."

"That's great."

"You'll be okay with the kids, right?"

"Yeah. Miss you."

"Miss you, too." The words stalled in her throat.

"See you when you get back."

"Okay." Before he hung up, she said, "Hey, Brian?"

"Yeah, babe."

"I'm not fully committed to staying 'til Saturday; I just wanted to give you a heads up."

The flight landed in the Birthplace of Aviation on time. Rachel rolled her carry-on past baggage claim. She sat in her car and vacillated between being Cat Woman and Brian's wife. The monologue mirrored a cartoon with the little red devil on the left shoulder and an angel on the right.

"I can't do this. Brian is a good man."

"I know he is."

"So why am I contemplating this rendezvous with Conrad?"

"Because you're empty."

"But that's selfish. I promised to love, honor and forsake all others."

"In your forsaking, who's taking care of you?"

"Conrad."

"So why deny yourself? It's your turn to be happy."

"I do deserve to be happy. Besides, we're just going to talk."

"Like at the office."

"It's not like we're going to have sex."

"Exactly. You are in control."

"And I'm not that kind of woman; never have been."

"And you're not going to start now."

She put the key in the ignition and then exited the long-term parking lot. When she approached the highway access, she panicked. A simple turn of the steering wheel could change her life forever. Veering to the right would take her home to her family and status-quo life. A move to the left would place her on the path to excitement, intrigue and fulfillment.

Undecided and at the fork in the road, she pulled over onto the shoulder and then stared at the highway sign. In her mind, Vandalia looked like imprisonment and Interstate 70 East to Dayton was liberation. She clenched her hands around the steering wheel, squeezed and then closed her eyes. She tried to remember when she last felt a smidgen of satisfaction with Brian. How long had it been since they laughed out loud over a joke? When was the last time they tussled playfully on the floor or raced down the stairs? Why did they stop talking *to* each other and start talking *at* each other? When did she stop loving her husband? When did she become indifferent toward him?

Her mind and heart were at war. Logic dictated that choosing Brian and the children was the only rational decision. No quandary, no dilemma. Go home. But her heart; her heart wasn't convinced. Her heart longed for passion, pleasure and Conrad. It yearned for the nuance of romantic love, the thrill of discovery.

The more she thought about Conrad, the more her body responded. Imagining his touch caused her heart to race. His smell consumed her, made her light-headed. The sweat on her palms made her hands slide off the steering wheel.

She checked the rearview mirror, flipped on her signal of intent, merged onto the airport access road. Vying for the

238

more scenic route, she headed to the hotel.

As she navigated through the construction barrels on Interstate 75 south, she thought about her father; the first to sever her heart. She recalled how he used to toss her in the air and then catch her just before she hit the ground. He protected her, loved her, left her. And Donald, the first man to whom she relinquished her uninhibited intimacy. She loved him, cherished him—only to have him betray her without apology or explanation. Brian, the faithful, committed man who never left her side, but left her uncovered. Left her vulnerable, afraid, unprotected and susceptible.

She pulled into the parking garage, drove to the upper level for isolated discretion and then parked in the southernmost corner. She turned off the car, fumbled with the keys. She picked them up off the floor, reached for her purse. *What's that room number again?*

Her stomach rumbled. She blamed it on hunger, but knew that it was nervous jitters. *If this is so wrong, then why am I having spasms and splashing down below? Why am I short of breath?*

Rachel rode the elevator to the corridor which connected the Dayton Convention Center to the Crowne Plaza. She looked down onto Jefferson Street and wondered how many of the commuters were in love. How many of them had been bombarded with passion? Enamored? She saw a man running after a lady's hat that had been whipped off her head by a gust of wind.

The second-floor entry off the corridor permitted her to enter the hotel without passing through the lobby. She noticed her hand trembling as she pressed the elevator call button. She clasped her hands together to still the anxiety. *What am I doing?*

She stepped into the elevator—the portal of no return—pressed the third-floor button and then bowed her head. The vertical one-story journey seemed to be a jaunt through a black hole. On the other side of this doorway, lay another world. A galaxy far removed from her current planet of inhabitation. With an alien life form that had the ability to read her mind, create something out of nothing and tap into the great unknown: the abyss of hopeful love.

The doors opened. Paralyzed with uncertainty and fear of the unknown, Rachel watched as the doors closed.

"If this elevator doesn't move by the time I count to ten, I'm meeting with Conrad." She counted to ten throwing in two Mississippis between each number. No movement. She counted to twenty, then fifty. Nothing. She pressed the button to open the doors and then stepped out of the elevator.

She shortened her stride, focused her eyes on the pattern in the carpet. Vertigo. She leaned on the wall to steady herself.

"Shake it off, girl. You're a grown woman acting like a girl with a grade-school crush." The quirkiness was foreign to the analytical corporate mogul who subverted emotions to get the job done. She took a deep breath, traced her hand on the wall, walked to destiny.

"Three thirteen. Three fifteen. Three seventeen." She paused, sighed. "Three nineteen."

She stared at the room number mounted on the door and then bowed her head. *I can't believe I'm standing at the threshold of adultery. How did I get here?* She tried to raise her hand to knock on the door, but the weight of indecision made it too heavy. She rubbed her hands together and then touched the door like a thief trying to open a safe.

Ever so softly, she knocked thrice, waited. *Maybe he's not here.*

As she turned to walk away, Conrad opened the door.

I invite you to continue your experience with

The Forbidden Secrets of the Goody Box!

Complete the *Reading Group Guide* on page 247

And visit

TheGoodyBoxBook.com

- Share how you feel about *The Forbidden Secrets of the Goody Box* and read what others are saying.
- Post your insights about men and dating and discuss the book with other readers at The Goody Box Forum.
- Chat online with me.
- Purchase additional copies of *The Forbidden Secrets of the Goody Box*.
- Join the Goody Box Club to learn about the sequel, prequel, audio books and the Uterus Adventures. These weekend excursions are exclusively for women. They are designed to relax, rejuvenate and refresh mind, body and soul by incorporating workshops, candid discussions and thrill-seeking, exhilarating adventures.
- Find out the latest news on The Goody Box Project.

This book can become a *New York Times* Bestseller with the help of passionate readers who want to pass it along to others.

If you are as moved by the message of *The Forbidden Secrets of the Goody Box* as I am, you may have come up with some creative ways to share your experience. To assist you with sharing this book with others, here are some ideas I refer to as

THE
Goody Box
PROJECT

Give the book to family, friends and strangers as a gift. Not only will they get page-turning entertainment with Debra, Rachel and Sherry, but also a wonderful glimpse into the mind of men that few women enjoy.

If you have a website or blog, share a bit of the book and how it touched you. Don't give away the plot, but recommend that they read it and then link to TheGoodyBoxBook.com.

Write a review for your local paper, favorite magazine or website and Amazon.com. Ask your favorite radio show to have Valerie as a guest. Media people often give consideration to the requests of their listeners.

If you own a business, consider displaying books on your counter to resell to customers. Business owners and individuals who are gift givers can acquire books at a discounted rate. Volume-discount pricing is available for orders of six books or more. Great for book clubs!

Buy books as gifts to students, women ministries, battered women's shelters, prisons and other groups where the people might be encouraged by the message.

Talk about the book on email lists, forums and social networking sites. Don't make it an advertisement, but rather share how this book affected your life and offer a link to the site.

TheGoodyBoxBook.com

Why He Left You for Her Workshop

All eyes are on you as you make slow orchestrated steps toward the altar. The splendor of your tailored gown is magnified by the beaded embellishments. Your hair and makeup, perfect. The eloquently arrayed bouquet of fresh-cut flowers bombards your senses. For a brief moment, you stop, close your eyes, inhale the fragrance. The pianist seems to stroke the keys in sync with your racing heart. You open your eyes and gaze down the aisle to see the groom poised, ready to meet his bride. A full smile washes across your face, steadies your breathing. As you walk toward him, acknowledging each friend and family member with a glance, slight grin and head nod, you whisper a prayer to the Lord.

"Father, I thank You for this beautiful day. Everything is coming together as planned; even the weather is perfect. I ask Your grace upon this union that it may flourish. I have one question: When will it be my turn as bride? I'm happy for my girl, but… I'm tired of being alone, crying myself to sleep. Smiling at every man I meet, hoping; praying that he's the one. I love my nieces and nephews, but I'm ready to be a mother. The official has shot the gun to start the foot race and I'm stuck in the blocks watching my girlfriends run ahead with husbands in tow. Why am I still single? What is it about me that keeps me on this side of matrimony?"

Limousines, receiving lines and head tables! Phooey!

Had enough of being a hostess, bridesmaid or maid of honor?

Let me be bold, blunt and to-the-point on something most men would never dare tell a woman: you have more power to have men eating out of the palm of your hand than you realize. However, when it boils down to it either you know *The Forbidden **SECRETS** of the Goody Box* or you don't. And most women don't have a clue as to how to utilize the power they already posses. If that describes you, then don't worry because it's not your fault! You've just never been taught the TRUTH about what men really CRAVE in a woman and it requires **VERY LITTLE EFFORT** on your part!

Now I have some good news and some bad news. First, the bad news: What I'm going to unveil in my *Why He left You for Her Workshop* will make lots of the wrong kinds of men VERY upset! The good news: They are going to be upset because I will peel back the curtain and reveal to YOU all of the SECRETS you were never given about men.

In this workshop, you will discover:

- Three things that lead you to make terrible relationship decisions
- Every man's private marriage checklist
- A simple two-letter word that makes him want to pop the question
- Why he just won't propose
- Little signs that tell you he's the one
- How to become a "man" whisperer with advice from men you'd be crazy to ignore

Valerie is available to speak to your book club, school, church or organization. Whether it's a ten-minute presentation or a full-day workshop, this expert will encourage, inspire and empower your group to lock that box! For additional information, visit TheGoodyBoxBook.com, ValerieJLColeman.com or call 888.802.1802.

Reading Group Guide

for

The Forbidden Secrets of the Goody Box

1. If your objective is a committed relationship, it's important that you have a list of must-haves and preferences before your emotions are activated. Capture your expectations below:

Must-Haves: _____

_____

_____

_____

_____

_____

_____

_____

_____

Preferences: _____

_____

_____

_____

_____

_____

_____

_____

_____

2. List characteristics of each of the four types of hunters.

Predator: _____

_____

_____

_____

_____

Ambusher: _____

_____

_____

_____

_____

Parasite: _____

_____

_____

_____

_____

Companion: _____

_____

_____

_____

_____

_____

_____

3. What hunter tactics have been used to get to your goody box?

_____

_____

_____

_____

_____

4. What significance do "Daddy dates" have to daughters? You?

_____

_____

_____

_____

_____

5. Gary Chapman identified how we receive and express love in his book *The Five Love Languages*. Rank your love languages in importance, with 1 being most important.

_____ Quality Time

_____ Acts of Service

_____ Words of Affirmation

_____ Gifts

_____ Physical Touch

6. Having identified your primary and secondary love languages, what things can you put in place to ensure that a predator or ambusher doesn't "catch you off guard"?

_____

_____

_____

_____

_____

7. Women process attraction in the order of eyes-heart-goody box. How does that differ from men?

_____

_____

_____

_____

_____

8. What element is required to ensure that the relational process extends beyond a wham-bam-thank-you-ma'am encounter? Why do women find it difficult to implement?

_____

_____

_____

_____

_____

9. What are some signs of an emotional affair?

_____

_____

_____

_____

_____

10. Why does Rachel feel justified in seeking refuge with Conrad?

_____

_____

_____

_____

_____

11. While in Jamaica, Rachel shared that she had gotten quiet on God. What, if anything, has caused you to get quiet on Him?

_____

_____

_____

_____

_____

About Valerie J. Lewis Coleman

Valerie J. Lewis Coleman has helped thousands of women find relational fulfillment. With over twenty years of experience in family and relationships, Valerie explains how to avoid seventy percent of men who only want the goody box and what it takes to win the heart of Mr. Right-For-You. She shares how she overcame personal struggles and offers proven techniques to help you get off the crazy cycle of relational demise!

As the bestselling author of *Blended Families An Anthology*, Valerie has helped families navigate the challenges of child support, visitation, discipline and more. This expert has given advice on baby-momma drama, defiant children and disapproving in-laws. On her journey to assist others with building strong families, she shares her testimony and provides proven techniques to help you stop the stepfamily madness in your home!

This expert and award-winning publisher has helped aspiring authors from across the world navigate the challenges of self-publishing. With over ten years of experience in the book business, she divulges industry secrets on avoiding the top five mistakes made by new authors, pricing your book to sell and identifying dishonest publishers. Her dynamic presentation and knowledge of the business takes writers from pen to paper to published as they master self-publishing to make money!

ValerieJLColeman.com
PenOfTheWriter.com
QueenVPublishing.com

Pen of the Writer

*Out of Ephraim was there a root of them against Amalek; after thee, Benjamin, among thy people; out of Machir came down governors, and out of Zebulun they that handle the **pen of the writer**.*
~ Judges 5:14

Pen Of the WritER

is a publishing company committed to using the writing pen as a weapon to fight the enemy and celebrate the good news of Christ Jesus.

With over ten years of experience, Pen of the Writer prides itself on providing literary services for novice writers and published authors including

Queen V Publishing
Passionate Pens
Writing and Publishing Conferences
Coaching and Consultation

Pen of the Writer
Taking writers from pen to paper to published!

Pen of the Writer, LLC
Dayton, Ohio
PenOfTheWriter.com

Valerie J. Lewis Coleman

Blended Families An Anthology

An Amazon.com Bestseller!
By Valerie L. Coleman
ISBN-13: 978-0-9786066-0-2

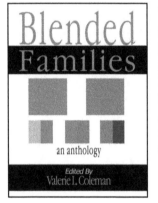

With divorce, single-parent households and family crises on the rise, many people are experiencing the tumultuous dynamics of blended or stepfamilies. Learn biblical principles and practical tools to help your family thrive. ***Blended Families An Anthology*** ministers to the needs of those hurting and crying out for answers.

*We are **not** the Brady Bunch!*
Stop the stepfamily madness!

Tainted Mirror An Anthology

By Valerie L. Coleman
ISBN: 978-0-9786066-1-9

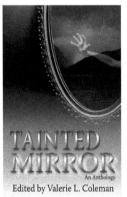

Whether restricted by prison walls, the influence of others or held hostage by self-inflicted limitations, captivity starts in the mind. We allow our thoughts to create virtual restrainers that stifle our dreams and hinder our purpose.

Based on I Corinthians 13:12, ***Tainted Mirror An Anthology*** offers stories of hope and healing to overcome the mental, physical and emotional strongholds that keep you from fulfilling your destiny.

What's keeping you from your destiny?

Available on **Amazon.com** and **PenOfTheWriter.com**

For speaking engagements or to order additional copies of

The Forbidden Secrets of the Goody Box

Pen of the Writer, LLC
893 South Main Street – PMB 175
Englewood, Ohio 45322
PenOfTheWriter.com
888.802.1802

* * * * * * * * * * * * * * * * * *

Name
_____

Address
_____

City / State / Zip
(_____)_____
Phone

E-mail
_____

Quantity	Price Per Book	Total
	$14.95	
Sales Tax (OH residents add $1.05 per book)		
Shipping ($3.99 first book, $0.99 each additional)		
Grand Total* (Payable to: Pen of the Writer)		

* Certified check and money orders only

Also available on Amazon.com in paperback and Kindle!
Nook, Sony Reader and other e-book formats at
SmashWords.com/Books/View/20787

.

CPSIA information can be obtained
at www.ICGtesting.com
Printed in the USA
BVHW08s2125060618
518374BV00006B/93/P